TIRZAH MM HAWKINS

Trusting the Enemy

Book One of The Monarch's Daughter

First published by Tirzah MM Hawkins 2024

First edition

This book was professionally typeset on Reedsy.
Find out more at reedsy.com

Contents

1

Read Me First

Thank you for buying my story! I appreciate you so much.

The Monarch's Daughter was first published as a serial story on Kindle Vella and is currently ongoing with no scheduled end. Buckle up for a dark, wild, epic ride.

Each season of The Monarch's Daughter will be published for readers who wish to read only eBooks and/or paperbacks, though you'll have to wait a bit for each one to be released. I'm writing as quickly as I can.

I'm leaving this edition of the story in serial format for several reasons. It benefits those of you who don't want to wait for the next installment to be published. You'll be able to know what episode you are on if you ever want early access by reading on my subscription platform. So many people can't wait for the next chapter and would rather read weekly as I write it.

You can find more information about early access to my work, my subscription, my book box offerings, and everything else you might want to know about me here: Tirzah-

MMHawkins.com.

Thank you for reading! I hope you enjoy this dark fantasy tale of mine as much as I enjoy writing it!

* * *

Content warning: There is a lot of controversy concerning content warnings. From my interactions in the reading community, I see almost an even split over whether or not people want content warnings. Here's what I will say in hopes of appeasing both sides. This piece of fiction is a very dark fantasy story. If you are easily disturbed or triggered, then this story and most of my writing probably aren't for you.

You can find a lot of specific warnings in the reviews for the story.

* * *

Early readers asked for a pronunciation guide.

Senice (Sen-ISS)

Flynae (Flih-NAE)

Thyde (Tide)

Issiah (ih-SIGH-uh)

Kaliah (kuh-LEE-uh).

2

Wedding Dream (Senice)

Senice walks through an avenue of trees, their leaves brilliant shades of red, orange, and gold. The way is familiar to him. He travels toward the chapel where he once wed a maiden so fair his heart aches with the memories of her.

She is now long gone.

Fresh air, clean and uncorrupted by modern technology, fills his nose with its sweet scent. Birds serenade the forest from the overhead branches. The nearby critters do not flee from him but rather creep closer, drawn to his pleasing aura. A gangly fawn follows him down the dirt path.

The structure appears ahead, looking the same now as the day the Kaliah created it almost four millennia ago. Seeing it again carries him back to the day when he assisted the others in the creation of it. They blessed it and the surrounding grove to remain untouched for as long as the home planet exists.

Each afternoon the sunlight filters down through the trees feeding the flowers and making the green meadow glow. The grass and nearby flowers exist in a perpetual state of manicured yet wild-crafted beauty.

The chapel, a one-story building with a tall, slanted roof, is made from the wood of the trees growing around it. The outside glows with a warm maple color and trim accents of deep cherry.

Two beings are within, but one of them stands out. Her aura sings with joy, overshadowing a timidity or nervousness that most others would miss. Senice's soul ignites with delight at her presence and wants to dance with her.

When he opens the door, his delicate ears detect the rustle of leaves created by the air movement, and he steps inside. Across the open room sits a maiden in her wedding dress. On her head rests a crown of branches intertwined with ivy and soft pink and white flowers. He recognizes the elven part of her from living amongst them in his youth, though pure elves vacated this galaxy four thousand years ago.

The girl is a young Kaliah of no more than eighteen or nineteen years. Her ruby red hair and emerald green eyes, dual traits of the royal family, match his.

Senice's breath catches in his throat at her beauty. He wonders who is allowing her to marry at such a tender age and who the lucky Kaliah boy is. May he be deserving of her.

She looks up as he enters; her eyes light up and a smile graces her elegant face. His heart skips a beat.

"Senice," the maiden calls out in a musical voice, rising to her feet.

His name affectionately dropped from her lips is one of the most pleasant sounds he's heard and warms him to his soul.

She runs toward him, twirling once. Iridescent fabric flows in an arc around her as she giggles and races into his awaiting arms.

Then she's in his embrace, and he doesn't know if he'll be able to let her go. She's precious to him.

"You look happy, dear one." He kisses her forehead beneath her ornately braided hair.

She looks up with her large glittering feline eyes. "I am."

"Good. You deserve every happiness, Flynae." A single tear escapes his eye, though it's unusual for a Kaliah to weep.

"Don't cry, Uncle Senice." She caresses his cheek with her silken hand. Delight blooms across her face the moment her eyes leave his to look at the entrance.

"My groom is here." Her cheeks turn an endearing shade of red. "I should go."

With great reluctance, he releases her. His stunning niece dances and twirls back to the private room at the far end of the chapel.

A soft breeze kisses his bare arms, as the door behind him opens. He turns with curious anticipation of who the lucky Kaliah is that won his niece's heart.

Joyfulness morphs to confusion and trepidation when a human enters.

"Emperor Thyde," he says, inclining his head. A knowing inside him tells him this is but a dream, a vision of things that may come to pass. Still, he is confused. Why this human? And how?

"Senice." The man returns the respectful motion. "How is she?" His attention shifts to the door hiding his bride.

"You know her state of mind better than I do. Her scent is a whirlwind of excitement and nerves. Yet she's the very definition of grace and beauty, absolutely stunning." His breath catches with pride.

A smile brightens the man's face reaching his eyes. Devotion exudes from his pores.

At that moment, the Kaliah is assured the man would give his life for Flynae. Peace washes his worry away.

The two of them walk as friends, side by side, from the chapel. A stepping stone path leads them around the side to a clearing. Trees line the opening and form a green canopy with their branches. Two figures stand waiting, one a human woman, the other a young Kaliah lad a little older than the maiden.

Senice wonders how long in the future this reverie might be. In present time, the Kaliah boy, Fennec, is but a lad of six. In the dream, he presents as being in his mid-twenties, still young, yet fully grown.

Senice takes his place beneath the trees and realizes from where he stands, he is conducting the ceremony. Momentarily, a black-haired Kaliah girl exits the chapel and joins Cellyna and Fennec to one side.

He stares at her in confusion. Her features are identical to the red-haired bride in many ways except for her raven hair and yellow eyes. The bride is shorter and of a smaller build, a little more dainty and fragile than her twin.

With anticipation, the small group waits for the bride, but she does not come.

Emperor Thyde leans toward him and whispers, "She's asking for you."

He hastens back wondering what she requires of him. Her delicate face peeks out through the doorway. A smile enhances her demeanor when he comes into view.

"Flynae, what is it?"

"There's no way I can walk out by myself."

The corners of his lips lift in an involuntary smile. She is serious, and her bashfulness is endearing.

"All right, dear one." He holds out his elbow.

Flynae intertwines her arm with his, and he escorts her. She clings to him and presses against him, never releasing her hold until she takes her groom's arm.

Senice reclaims his place before them and witnesses the bride and groom looking into each other's eyes. Peace floods his body. Whatever led him to this day reassures him they belong together.

He murmurs in his native tongue. The words flow out in a melody. A warm ball of light blossoms and grows from the couple's intertwined hands. It starts no larger than a dot and increases until the couple is enveloped by it.

As the ceremonial rite reaches completion, the vision vanishes into darkness.

Senice wakes from his dream as six-year-old Fennec, his nephew, runs into the room shouting, "The babies are coming."

3

Death (Flynae)

"Flynae, wait here." Issiah, her father, forcefully nudges her toward a doorway. Something in his voice compels her to obey. Worry creases his forehead and narrows his eyes as he kneels to be on a similar level with her. Warm hands pull her hood up over her head and caress her face.

A deep dread creeps over her, leaving her skin prickling in its wake. She swallows hard and glances from his bright emerald feline eyes, the same shade and shape as hers, to the street ahead of them.

This part of the city holds the old-world charm of ages almost forgotten from long ago, a stark contrast to the modern skyscrapers and architecture just a couple miles away. The brick and wooden houses lining the cobblestone streets sit a wide enough distance apart to welcome pedestrians, but near enough to each other to deter all but single-rider vehicles to enter, leaving the alleyway a pleasant, welcoming place for those on foot to escape the noisy bustle of the capital.

Today, a shadow casts icy fingers over the normally warm and inviting area. Ripples from an advancing darkness issue forth and hit her body like violent shockwaves.

Her breath quickens. With the gift and curse of an inhuman wisdom beyond her short four years, she recognizes something is different.

For several months, she's walked these streets twice a week with her father, without incident, to dance lessons. Despite fighting to keep calm, panic grips her chest with an iron fist. Since her birthday three months ago, her gift of sight keeps growing, the images and premonitions becoming clearer and more frequent.

"Peace, Flynae," Issiah whispers a Kaliah boon to her. "All will be well." The corners of his lips turn up, softening his face in a painfully beautiful way.

She smiles, tremulously in response, though tears well in her eyes. One spills down her cheek.

He wipes away the rogue drop. "No crying in front of humans, my daughter." His voice is kind yet stern.

She nods and rubs the extra moisture from her face. His eyes shine his approval. A tightness twists her gut.

This is goodbye.

While her father might not understand the depth of the situation, her sight whispers an undeniable premonition. And lately, her premonitions, good or bad, come true.

Flynae lowers her head and closes her eyes asking in their kind's tradition for a blessing. Her father places his hands on either side of her head and kisses her forehead.

She inhales his scent, burning it into her memory. Though her whole body trembles, she tells herself he must know what is best. Huddling back into the doorway, she hides in the shadows as best she can.

The distance between them widens to a chasm as he leaves

her. He walks down the street. Before he's out of sight, he stops and waits.

This isn't right. She looks down at her hands which were just moments ago disguised to appear human by her father's energy. The protection is now tenuous. Her fingertips flash back and forth in front of her from short, manicured nails to long, sharp Kaliah claws.

Knowing she must be quiet, she stifles a cry. Her father's abilities have never failed no matter how far apart they were.

As if he sensed her increasing alarm, his gaze turns back toward her. His mouth pressed together in a flat line, his features showing distress and hesitancy for the first time.

He isn't well.

The thought nagged at her when they first left, and she wanted to insist that they remain home.

Issiah lifts a finger to his face and purses his lips, and she realizes her breaths are coming in loud, ragged gasps.

I must be calm.

Last week, her father started her energy training, teaching her how to wield the power that flows through and around them. Controlling emotions is the foundation upon which the rest builds. She draws on the natural life forces surrounding her to assist her in slowing her breathing.

The sound of her breath fades, giving way to thudding footsteps that reverberate through her ears and into her being.

The man approaching them exudes confidence. He entertains no doubts about the success of his mission. From the growing booms of his every step, he is close and will soon appear from around the corner.

Each footfall brings doom closer.

He means to harm my father.

Once the thought sprouts, she can't deny its truth. Icy fingers of dread claw at her insides. The impending presence of this powerful human when her father is weaker than she ever thought possible is no coincidence.

If only I were Fennec right now.

Her brother, seven years her elder, has seven years of training on her. Fennec knows how to use a lifesword, and might even be old enough to hold his own against a human.

The footsteps ring louder in her sensitive hearing. She claps her hands over her tall elf-like ears to block as much of the grim sound as she can.

The owner of the footfalls appears, striding in the direction of her father with purpose. The floor-length cape flowing behind him, combined with his head-to-toe black attire, denotes him as a lord in this galaxy.

Without hesitating, he advances toward her father. In his hand, he grips a foot-long metal cylindrical pipe. From it springs five feet of narrow condensed blue light energy, no more than two inches in diameter.

Flynae gasps. Humans aren't supposed to possess the gift to control energy and wield a lifesword the way Kaliah can.

Issiah removes his lifesword hilt, a bare piece of wood resembling a torch handle, from his belt. In answer to the human, he lights his flaming brand, reddish-orange like fire in color.

Her fingers clench into a fist, wishing she was allowed to wear her lifesword so she could fight beside her father. But she isn't permitted to carry a weapon that she isn't adept at manipulating.

The human strikes first, and her father blocks. Her keen eyes notice the glow of her father's lifesword weakens. The energy blade won't last much longer.

Her stomach twists and her breath catches in her throat as she searches her brain for something she can do. Her father should be able to best any human without breaking a sweat. He is the Monarch of the Kaliah, the strongest of their kind, and more powerful than any human.

Issiah advances a step, and her confidence in him returns but only for a moment. The human sees the opening in A deep dread creeps over her, leaving her skin prickling in its wake. She swallows hard and glances from his bright emerald feline eyes, the same shade and shape as hers, to the street ahead of them.eep into his torso nearly severing him in half.

All her father's warnings fly from her memory, and she forgets she is supposed to remain hidden. A scream of horror escapes her lips, straining her lungs.

"Father!" She dashes out, ignoring the human, in order to catch her father's head before it hits the cobblestones.

A brief moment of recognition flashes in her father's eyes as his hand reaches out to touch her face once more. Then his energy slips away.

Flynae grasps at his life force, trying to pull it back into his body, to no avail. His eyes close. She isn't skilled enough to save him.

"No," she screams, clutching at his inert form. "Father. Stay with me."

4

Death (Kovad)

The severed Kaliah collapses before him.

"Father!" A shrill voice screams. A small female form races to the dying male's side, her head covered in long waves of blood-red hair, the same color as the scarlet flowing from her father's body.

"No! Father," the little being whispers the name the second time as she attempts to catch the body before it can fall to the ground. The weight pulls her to her knees. "Stay with me."

Anger flares within Lord Kovad Thyde. He'd been deceived. Worse. He was lied to. His orders were to eliminate any witnesses, though he'd been assured in the next breath the alley would be deserted.

Kovad raises his lifesword again and grabs the girl's shoulder. Her head whips up. Her feline eyes, brilliant green like her father's, pierce his soul.

He blinks repeatedly, coming to a heightened awareness like awakening from a dream or trance.

At that moment, he's both staring down at her and looking back up at himself. Every feature about him is evaluated and memorized in an instant– his stormy-blue eyes; dark raven hair; strong, square jaw; and tall, muscular build.

A hint of fear registers upon documenting his raised arm, but a grief and heartache that will never diminish overpower the alarm and sweep it away.

A sour, sweet aroma, identified as adrenaline, assaults his senses. How does he know what to call it?

Something, or someone, labeled it; and he distinctly heard their thought in his mind.

The pounding of his heart in his head echoes, forming two distinct, racing beats.

As the vision of his face in a mirror doesn't fade, he realizes with awe that the girl before him witnesses herself through his eyes with no way to explain how. She notes that her human disguise faded to allow her tall, slender ears to peek through her deep red hair. In the bright morning light, the oval irises of her eyes constrict to no more than slits of black in a sea of glittering emerald. Amid these vibrant colors lies a porcelain white face.

Oh, gods. He sees me.

The child's voice registers in his mind as clearly as if she spoke the words aloud, but her lips never moved.

Shame takes a prominent position in the forefront of her feelings as she tries in vain to stop the tears spilling down her face. In her anguish, she failed her father's last request.

A tear leaks down Kovad's face. While his skin tracks the motion, he watches it from a vantage point outside his body as well.

All the confidence and pride building within him throughout the morning from being entrusted with the top-secret mission from the Emperor now morphs to regret and confusion. His emotions mix with hers into one muddy, overwhelming wave.

His elevated arm falters and lowers

Through eyes that are not his own, he sees a line on his cheek, clear as day, where his tear traveled.

The girl wipes her face, ridding herself of the evidence of her failing.

Kovad extinguishes his lifesword and returns the hilt to his belt. With one more astonished, bewildered glance at the Kaliah girl, he turns and strides from her view, his footfalls lacking the authority with which he'd arrived.

He marches almost blindly down the empty streets before him, barely seeing the buildings he passes as multiple scenes collide and overlap in his mind. The memory of striking down the Kaliah doubles into two different views, the one he saw from his eyes as well as the one she saw from hers.

Issiah's lifeless face lies at the center of his mind, but he's looking at it through eyes that detect more details than he has ever seen. Even through the fresh tears blurring her vision.

5

Found (Flynae)

Flynae wipes her eyes and curses herself for displaying weakness in front of a human.

The man recalls the energy flowing from his hand back into his body, extinguishes his lifesword, and returns the hilt to his belt. He meets her eyes once more, and she's painfully aware of how substantial her feline eyes register in his mind as she sees them through his eyes.

The sight doesn't surprise or shock him. Without knowing how, she realizes he's met a Kaliah before, an adult male.

Awe at her beauty washes from him into her. Her charm, as a female Kaliah child, is beyond any he's experienced in a being. With a scent of sorrow and regret, he pivots and walks away, all power and charge absent from his movements.

Flynae turns back to her father's body and more tears fall unbidden from her eyes. Not wanting another human to happen upon her crying, she wipes them away.

Desiring help, she glances around. At this time of day, people should be present on the street. Even at her young age, she understands someone orchestrated this situation. For months now, the two of them traversed this path to her dance lessons, and never did she see it empty. Whoever planned this didn't want spectators. Now, no one lingers nearby to assist her.

Every glance at her father's lifeless face inflicts a deep wound in her memory that won't ever ebb.

The Kaliah inherited the elven trait for impeccable retention. Once old enough to make intelligent, cognitive decisions— between two and three years of age— a Kaliah never forgets anything. Sensations and happenings do not fade in time the way they do in the human mind.

She will remember the image of her father being struck a mortal blow and the accompanying heartache as poignantly and vividly in a millennium as she does experiencing it now.

Flynae lifts her father's hand and sets it in her lap. Around his wrist, he wears a small comm device. In desperation, she presses a few buttons.

Issiah never instructed her on its use though. After several frustrating, frantic moments of achieving nothing, she gives up and lies down in the crook of his arm. With her head on his chest, she notices his body heat fading and prays someone friendly comes along soon.

Strong arms lift and clutch her.

Flynae blinks away sleep from her eyes and finds the sun nearing the apex of the sky.

Her Uncle Senice holds her. She encircles his neck with her arms and weeps.

"I'm so sorry, dear one," he whispers into her ear, his lips close enough that they brush her skin.

The presence of five other Kaliah registers in her awareness before they enter her sight. Four of them lovingly lift Issiah's body and set it on a width of cloth attached to two wooden poles to carry him between them.

Underneath the mourning, the nervous energy of the group tightens like a vice around her. Every Kaliah answered to Issiah as their Monarch. Which royal will rise to take his place?

Flynae wishes for her oldest brother, whom she's never met, to appear and claim the position; but no one's heard from Siah for a millennium. He disappeared into hiding long ago with a small band of Kaliah sworn to protect Warah, Siah's wife and the last full-blooded elf in the galaxy.

The final Kaliah with them is Eksar. Flynae knows him as her uncle though his lack of blood relations to her and Senice is apparent in his midnight black hair and deep yellow eyes. Those wolf eyes study her now as she clings to Senice's neck.

For the first time ever, her insides squirm under the watchfulness of his gaze.

6

Voice (Flynae)

"What do you mean, you're keeping *both* the girls?" Senice seethes.

Flynae and Sekara sit clutching each other on one of the beds in their shared bedroom while their Uncle Senice argues with his stepbrother, Eksar, a floor beneath them. The twin girls are mirror images in every way except that Sekara does not have the royal traits: her hair is jet black, her eyes golden yellow.

Their keen ears allow them to hear every word, every intonation as if they were in the room with the adults.

"You heard me," Eksar mutters in a low tone.

The girls recoil and tremble at the hatred in his voice. Flynae had always been hypersensitive to Eksar's contempt for her father and Senice, though she never understood the reason for it.

"I can understand Sekara, but why Flynae?" Senice lowers his voice, possibly to sound more calming and reasonable or in hopes that the girls won't hear. "You care nothing for her."

Flynae finds sense in Senice's arguments. Eksar is always

doting over Sekara, taking her places, buying her things. He's never shown her the same affection.

"Oh, I care for her." Eksar's words have an undercurrent of maliciousness that sends a cold shiver down Flynae's spine. Sekara squeezes her sister even tighter. "I care that she is raised appropriately for her purpose in this life."

"Her purpose. What is your meaning?" The unease in Senice's voice is unmistakable.

All air leaves Flynae's lungs in a whoosh as she realizes that in just a matter of days she has lost her father and is now losing Senice and her brother, Fennec.

"Eksar?" A waiver in Senice's speech reveals a struggle to maintain his composure. "What have you done? Tell me you didn't have a hand in Issiah's death."

Even in the absence of words of response, Flynae feels the sense of a cold gloating smile on Eksar's face. The tension between the two adult males permeates through the floor. Suddenly, she is afraid for Senice.

Issiah had taught Flynae that a member of the royal family, The Monarch, would always be the strongest Kaliah in the galaxy. For the last four millennia, her father had been The Monarch. She knew that the royal gift had not passed to Senice. While much stronger than her because of his years, Senice was never a great fighter. If Eksar so chose, he could overwhelm and destroy Senice.

She leaps from the bed, extricating herself from her sister's grasp, and races down the stairs; her heart pounding in her ears is the only sound she hears. As Kaliah hardly make a sound when they walk or run, Flynae senses rather than hears Sekara follow her.

The situation hasn't escalated to fighting yet as the uncles glare at each other, but Flynae is all too aware that both their dominant lifesword hands are tense, ready to react if needed.

"Stop," she screams out. They both turn and look at the girls. Flynae runs to Senice and grips his leg. "I can't lose you, too."

Senice kneels and puts his arms around her while looking up imploringly at Eksar. "Don't make me leave her," he begs.

"The pitifulness from the two of you is annoying me. You will leave now, Senice. You may see her at the funeral in two days."

When Flynae turns and looks up at Eksar, there is no compassion in his eyes. For the second time in just a few days, she is frightened.

"Now," Eksar adds sternly.

Senice stiffens.

Flynae doesn't know if he means to comply or to fight. "Please," she whispers, "Just go. I'll be fine." She releases him and steps back as if to show him that she can be strong.

Senice places his hands on the sides of her head. She lowers her chin, and he kisses her forehead. "I'll see you soon." He sighs with a heavy heart. Flynae feels the weight of it pressing in on her small form, crushing her.

Instead of bending, she straightens, gathers her courage, and nods her head. If he senses how fearful she is right now, he'll never leave. She is a royal daughter and already knows how to suppress her emotions.

Slowly, Senice stands and withdraws from the house. When the door shuts behind him, Flynae pulls her eyes from it and steels herself to look at Eksar. His leer is harsh and triumphant as he meets her eyes.

"Go upstairs," he says roughly. "I don't want to see you until dinner."

Without a word, she makes her way silently and proudly, her head held high, to her bedroom, Sekara close behind her. The girls resume their place on the bed with their arms wrapped around each other. Their emotions mix. Flynae feels trepidation coursing through her; Eksar has never been affectionate or even cordial towards her. Sekara is concerned for her sibling though she does not fear Eksar.

The day passes slowly. Eventually, the twins each take up a book to pass the time, reading their own tomes side by side, shoulders touching, on the bed.

Hours later, Eksar calls them down for a dinner of raw steak and uncooked vegetables. Kaliah traditionally eat mostly raw or just lightly cooked foods. What would normally be delicious is ash in Flynae's mouth.

They eat dinner in silence, just the three of them. Flynae realizes that she has never been around Eksar without another adult present. His gaze is oppressive, severe towards her making her afraid, wishing she could vanish into the air. Even Sekara is unwilling to break the heavy silence.

Flynae mostly picks at her food. Her grief and trepidation have her stomach twisted into knots.

The dense energy affects Sekara as well. She doesn't eat much more than her twin.

Eksar doesn't seem to mind. He finishes his plate and tells the girls to put theirs away. The girls obey and quickly move to retreat to their bedroom. Eksar stands in Flynae's way.

"Not so fast."

Her eyes lift to meet his in question. Her body shivers.

"Follow me," he says to her. "Sekara, head upstairs and get ready for bed."

The girls exchange a wary glance before Flynae turns to

follow him downstairs into the basement. He leads her to the far end where he opens a door and stands to the side.

"In," he commands.

Flynae steps forward and sees before her a bare room with cement walls containing just a bed, dresser, and small closet. Eksar must have been preparing this all afternoon.

"The bathroom is across the hall. I expect you in bed in ten minutes." Without another word, he leaves her alone.

The basement is cold, but the energy around her feels warmer without his presence so near. She changes into some night clothes from the dresser and then makes her way across the hall to wash her face and bare feet for bed. She's barely back in the bedroom when all the lights downstairs go off at once. The sudden darkness overwhelms her, and she clamps her hands over her mouth to stifle a scream. While Kaliah have night vision like a cat's, they can't see anything if there is no light at all. The complete darkness is terrifying to her.

She draws up her legs to her chest and pulls the covers to her chin, her body trembling. *Don't cry; don't cry*, she begs herself to maintain control. The more she repeats it and scolds herself for her weakness, the less able she is to restrain herself. Hot tears roll down her cheeks as she begins to sob.

"What the fuck?" a deep male voice says loud and clear.

The voice startles her, and her crying jerks to a stop as she tries to listen for the origin. She turns her head from side to side unable to name the owner or detect a source. Her acute senses detect nothing else in the room with her unless it has no need to breathe or no life energy of its own. She extends her hearing out beyond the walls of the room. She can discern a nearby neighbor taking a shower and the many hearts beating of an earthworm on the other side of the concrete wall. But there is nothing she can sense indicating where the voice came from.

Did I imagine it? she wonders. At some point, her intense listening relaxes and she falls asleep.

7

Meditation (Flynae)

The next day, the girls do their best to remain quiet and out of sight, mostly hiding in their backyard treehouse with their favorite books. Their childhood home is the nicest in the cul-de-sac with a giant backyard compared to any of the others around them. You would never guess that the family was the wealthiest on the planet. Issiah wanted the girls to grow up knowing how to blend in with humans even as they were instructed to limit their emotional involvement with them.

Eksar spent most of the day in his study, the energy radiating from him penetrating even to the backyard was that of anger and frustration. The twins felt mutual trepidation when they were eventually called in for dinner.

Flynae wishes the floor would swallow her up when Eksar's glare falls over her as she sits down at the table. She painfully tries not to squirm in her seat as she attempts a few bites of dinner. Each swallow is like a rock sliding down her throat to land with a heavy thud in her stomach.

No one says anything for the full thirty minutes it takes Eksar to consume his dinner, his chewing methodical, his narrowed eyes never leaving Flynae. During that time, the rage she senses in him keeps building. Her thoughts are of hiding and escaping.

After swallowing his last bite, he drops his fork onto his plate with a clatter. He scrapes his chair back across the floor before standing. Sekara lets out a gasp. Flynae lowers her head as her shoulders rise. She knows something is coming that she is helpless to stop.

Eksar crosses the room in four long strides and grabs her hair. She throws up her hands to hold onto his arms and take some pressure off her scalp. He drags her from the room.

The sharp pain on her head holds most of her attention until her hip and legs bang down first one step and then another. A small cry escapes her lips. The dull pain becomes a burning sensation as he drags her across the cold cement basement floor.

Finally, he comes to a halt in the middle of the bedroom and releases her. One of her hands applies pressure to her head while the other hugs her knees to her chest. As the fear and pain envelop her, she fights back the sobs not wanting to give him the satisfaction. Still, little hitching noises escape.

Then she is alone.

Except she is not alone.

She is aware of another presence sensing her. Her breath catches in her throat as she focuses on this new being. The pain lessens as she becomes distracted. Little hairs on the back of her neck stand on end. The sensation of noticing someone noticing her is new, but she relaxes as the new presence doesn't seem hostile.

Flynae takes deep, quiet breaths as she listens for any

indication of what or where this new entity is. No one is in the room with her, yet something is very aware of her. Goosebumps run across her arms and legs.

Is it a ghost? she wonders. *No.* Strangely, she can feel the blood running through the being's veins as if she were outside herself in someone else's body. Its heartbeat thumps in her head. Though no one else is present, she hears a breath deeply inhaled and then exhaled loud and clear.

Are you okay?

The voice isn't audible, but she can hear it as clearly as if it were standing next to her. Or rather, as if it were standing *in* her.

The overhead lights go off.

She gasps, shuts her eyes, and climbs into the bed, pulling the covers around her as a shield against the darkness. The loss of ability to use one of her keen senses makes her feel vulnerable. Her palms sweat; her heart pounds within her. She has almost forgotten about the other presence as complete blackness overwhelms her. *I don't like this.*

Just breathe, the voice says soothingly. *Deep even breaths. The dark itself can't hurt you. Take a moment to listen. Do you hear anything?*

It's a man's voice talking to her. She's surprised by the calmness and gentleness in his voice. She's never heard the voice before, but she finds herself enjoying the sound of it. It's rich, deep, and controlled.

Her mind conjures a figure to go with it; someone tall with dark hair and a solid build. While the form is vague in her mind, she still gets enough of a sense of it to know he is too tall and muscular to be a Kaliah. Even the strongest of Kaliah are deceivingly slender; no one who didn't know what they were would ever guess their strength by looking at them.

After a moment to rein in her breathing and quiet it, she reaches out through her elf-like ears listening for sounds. There is little to hear though.

What do you feel in the energy around you? he asks.

Flynae knows enough about humans to know it is strange that one would be asking her about energy. All Kaliah and a very few humans are sensitive to the energy around them. It is not only a sixth sense but also something they can manipulate in certain ways. Senice and Issiah have trained her in energy control since she was old enough to walk. She taps into this sense now to see what life forms might be around her. There is nothing. She is alone. In all the basement she can find no other living energy except for that too small to be anything except insects. When she tries to connect to Sekara somewhere in the house above her, she finds that she can reach no further than the basement ceiling, which is strange. Never has she encountered such a limit before.

There is nothing nearby, she replies.

Then there is nothing near to hurt you.

These words are comforting. She relaxes back into her bed and sets her head on her pillow.

Who are you?

She hears him inhale and catch his breath on the exhale as if changing his mind. Then he sighs and contemplates another answer to her question.

Why don't you call me Kovad?

Kovad. Even his name is beautiful and reassuring. A name that a kind person would have. *Kovad. Why are you in my head, Kovad?* For a moment, she wonders if the darkness has truly made her go insane as she now talks to a voice in her head. But his essence is tangible, convincing her that he is real.

I don't know. I've been wondering the same thing myself. An image too brief for her to see flashes across his mind as if he has just had a thought and pushed it away. The memory, which she guesses the blip was, holds a painful quality in the something that he doesn't want her to see. His thoughts return to his breathing.

Well. I don't mind. I like you. He's been pleasant so far, and she appreciates the company in the stifling aloneness of the basement.

After another focused breath he thinks, *I don't deserve that.*

Flynae realizes that she heard his thought though it wasn't directed towards her. Melancholy tinges it.

Are you sad?

No, I'm not sad. He refocuses on controlling his breathing. *Just. Disappointed.* Two more thoughts that aren't directed at her come to his mind. *Angry. Betrayed.* He lets out his breath and clears his mind again.

His deep breathing prompts her to take a few of her own, relaxing her further. She yawns and realizes she is exhausted. Every minute since her father's death has been difficult.

Why don't you go to sleep now? His suggestion seems to come more from a place of kindness than of annoyance.

What is the breathing thing you are doing?

Meditating.

May I meditate with you? Until I fall asleep.

Sure.

8

Funeral (Flynae)

Flynae stares up at the bright patches of sapphire through the holes in the canopy of trees above her. The sunlight streams down in brilliant, warm rays, but the weather is unable to brighten her spirits. Her gaze moves to the ground beneath her, and she picks up another stick to add to the small bundle in her arms. Her cloak makes a soft rustling noise as it drags across the grass when she takes a step.

From the corner of her eye, she is aware of the adult Kaliah to her left gathering larger pieces of wood. He is just one of many Kaliah here today that she has never met before. They have all come to pay their final respects to her father.

She wonders how many of them have attended a Kaliah cremation before. It isn't common for a Kaliah to die. Her father was four millennia old and nowhere near dying of old age. Kaliah are said to be immortal, but she is now painfully aware of their mortality. Fear of losing the rest of her loved ones squeezes her chest like an icy fist. Only Senice, Fennec, and Sekara remain.

Senice passes by, carrying a large fallen tree trunk with another stranger. Her small armload of sticks won't add much to the fire, but she still needs to contribute to her father's funeral service.

She takes a deep breath of clean, crisp fall air. The leaves around her are in their full glory of brilliant gold and red hues, but she is numb to their beauty today.

Leftover raindrops from a recently passed storm fall from the branches. The sound mixes with the melancholy songs of the birds in the area. Nature senses the Kaliah's sorrow and mourns with them.

When her arms are full, she heads back to the clearing where the pyre has grown since the last time she saw it. They almost have enough wood to start the ceremony.

She hesitates, not wanting to carry her bundle forward and add it to the rest. If she does, it will solidify the moment as real instead of being some horrible nightmare she is trapped in and cannot awake from.

Flynae senses a nearby small life presence and glances down to see a large spider crawl from the wood onto her hand. She is not afraid. Her father taught her that nature does not harm Kaliah. It's better that the arachnid escape the wood now rather than be burned with her father's body. No more lives need to end.

As she lowers her hand to deposit the passenger on the ground, her keen eyes see, as if in slow motion, the spider raise its fangs and sink them into her flesh. Instantly, the venom courses through her arm, burning.

She screams, flinging her arm wildly until the spider flies off. The wood she held falls to her feet. Two red puncture wounds stand out from the marble flesh of her hand. *Why would it do that?*

Within a moment, Senice is kneeling at her side. He cups her hand, which is now beginning to swell around a large, red welt, between his. The venom, which has already crept up towards her shoulder, begins to retreat down her arm in answer to his pull.

Flynae trembles. This additional strain on an already stressful day is too much. Her mind replays the spider biting her over and over again with perfect recall.

"You're all right, dear one," he whispers lovingly. "What did this?"

Her confused eyes meet his concerned ones. "A spider. But why?"

Senice's eyes darken and narrow as they shift from hers to something behind her. She turns and sees Eksar standing at the edge of the clearing watching them, a pleased look on his face.

"It wasn't the spider's choice," Senice replies. He lets go of her hands, but she clutches his to hold him back.

"You can't," she pleads. "He'll kill you."

His frown softens when he turns back to her.

"I'm all right," she says managing a small smile. She twists her lie to a truth to make it more believable and holds out her hand which now shows no trace of the spider bite. "See?"

He glances at her hand and then back to her face. With all seriousness he says, "You tell me if he ever hurts you."

She resists the urge to bite her lip and give her thoughts away. "I will." She nods. "He won't." Her mind flashes back to Eksar pulling her down the stairs by her hair and how badly that hurt. Her legs are still bruised. But she can't tell Senice. The truth will get him killed. *I will learn to fight. I will become a warrior and kill Eksar myself.* This sounds plausible to her; she has royal blood within her while Eksar does not. This is a battle she will need to fight on her own.

Senice pulls her in and hugs her tightly. "You are very dear to me, Flynae."

"I know." She takes comfort in his embrace allowing him to share and relieve the most intense of her emotions.

All too soon, he stands up and releases her. "Let's finish this, shall we."

She nods and bends to pick up the sticks she dropped. This time she warefully checks them for spiders. Her heart pounds in her ears at the thought of finding another. The fangs sink into her skin anew, the memory as fresh in her mind as if it were happening again.

When she has reclaimed all the branches and has set her energy to repel any further arachnids, she carries them to the pyre and places them around the bottom with the rest of the kindling.

As she steps back, Senice takes her hand. They turn together to watch six Kaliah carry her father's body over on an intricately woven stretcher. The fabric is predominantly a rich black with a few strands here and there that shimmer and change color when you look at them. These are elven threads, extremely rare and precious. Kaliah cannot make such material as hard as they try to understand the enchantment of it. Flynae wonders if her brother's wife, Warah, has made these.

Issiah looks stately in kingly robes of emerald green. A crown of living branches braided and ornamented with golden flowers adorns his head.

The sight of her father's lifeless body takes Flynae back in time to just days prior when a man in black struck him down.

She smells the metallic of the cobblestones and blood. Her screams assault her ears as the lifesword flashes through the air. Once again, she is at his side trying to hold onto his life energy. For a moment, she is at once looking up at the man and seeing through his eyes looking back down at her. In the midst of all of this, she notices a sadness in the present that feels like it comes from the same place in her mind as Kovad's voice.

She blinks back her tears knowing that no matter how many millennia she lives, she'll never forget a single detail about that day. Perfect recall is a curse shared by elves and Kaliah alike: their memories never fade the way that humans do.

At least each passing day brings new memories to drown out the old. Distraction is a friend.

Fennec and Sekara return from the woods with their final loads of wood and stand with Senice and Flynae as Issiah's body is placed atop the pyre. Flynae takes her twin's hand while Fennec grasps Sekara's other hand.

The sun begins to set, but the fire won't be lit until it is fully dark.

Senice begins singing a traditional Kaliah dirge. The rest of the Kaliah join in by the second or third note. The songs continue into the night. Sometimes it is just one or two people singing; sometimes the only sound is a harp or flute playing.

The fire burns all night. By first light, the wood has all been consumed and just embers remain.

Without ceremony, Eksar approaches and beacons Sekara and Flynae. The girls comply, but Flynae doesn't miss the look that passes between her uncles. She silently prays that Senice will let her go for good, though she knows he never will.

Back at home in her basement bedroom, Flynae finds herself

exhausted yet unable to sleep. When she closes her eyes, she sees her father being struck down one minute and his body going up in flames the next.

Would you like some help? Kovad asks.

With what?

Going to sleep.

Yes. Please. She doesn't know how he can help her sleep, but she is thankful for the company.

All right. Get comfortable.

She adjusts her pillow and pulls another blanket over her. *Okay.*

Find a spot on the ceiling and focus on it.

She's relieved that he didn't ask her to close her eyes as she wouldn't be able to control what she saw. *Okay.*

Take deep slow breaths. All the way down into your belly. Hold. Exhale completely. Clench your fists. And relax them.

She enjoys the strain of clenching. Being tense is easy right now.

Now tense your shoulders, nice and tight. Then relax then. Deep, slow, complete breaths.

He directs her attention, tensing and relaxing, all the way down to her toes and then back up to her fists. His voice calms and soothes her.

When she yawns, he says, *Now close your eyes.*

She obeys and remembers no more as she falls asleep and sleeps without dreaming.

9

Mindlink (Kovad)

"I have never felt more exposed, more connected with someone in my life. The feeling is beyond words. I can't say for certain how it happened, but I know the moment it did. She was arguing with her boyfriend that night. I could hear them very clearly as I walked by, out for my evening stroll.

He was regularly abusive, but her screams that night were more terrified than I had ever heard before. Without much thought, I ran inside their apartment.

He had her bent over the kitchen table, his pants around his ankles. As she looked across the room at me, her eyes were wild with fear.

I pushed him off her, and she would have crumpled to the ground had I not pulled her into my arms. She looked up at me and suddenly I was looking at her through my eyes and myself through hers. I experienced all five of her senses. I felt her emotions; I could hear her thoughts.

With my support, she packed up and left town that night. We maintained our friendship until she passed away at the very human age of eighty-five. The experience of feeling someone die was painful and beautiful at the same time. It has been several hundred years since then, but I still miss her voice in my head." Author: Fulani.

Well, that wasn't helpful. Here's another one. Written by Senice Let. Seeing the name of a Kaliah he recognizes surprises him. *Really? How interesting. What were your thoughts on your 'mindlink', Senice?*

The name of her uncle being read in his head catches the attention of Flynae; he notices her paying attention as he continues reading.

"It's been exactly one thousand years since my Lucretia passed. She was my third human wife and will be my last. Kaliah never get over losing anyone the way that humans can, but most of them are blessed to never have to lose someone they were mindlinked with.

She was my best friend. We were unable to keep any secrets. She knew everything that had ever happened to me. Looking back, my deepest regret was not linking her life to mine. Issiah forbid it though. He holds no regard for humans, but I could have done it in secret. Siah may have even assisted me with it. He understands forbidden love with his Warah.

But now I'm left with regret and loss. The day she died was one of the darkest days in my memory. She wasn't in pain in the end at least. But I could feel her life energy slipping away, and I was helpless to stop it. I would have injected my blood into her veins if I had the tools to do so, another forbidden act. That would have prolonged her life a little, but to what end? The demise of us both?

Humans are mortals no matter how much they try not to be. I sat next to her and held her hand as her presence inside my head faded away. Kaliah tears are not for humans, but I wept over her when she was gone."

What are you doing? Flynae asks casually not wanting Kovad to realize she had been listening for a while without letting him know she was paying attention. It felt like spying.

Researching mindlinks. But there doesn't seem to be much information.

What do you want to know about them?

How to end it.

Flynae gasps from the sting of betrayal. Her mouth falls open. *But why?* She had resigned herself to being okay with the basement, and the dark, and missing her sister and Senice, because she had a friend. *Now he means to leave me, as well.*

Kovad sighs. *Because it's not fair to you. There are things about me that you don't want to know. There are things I do that you don't want to see. Having known you these few days, I would rather we part as friends than you hate me.*

She has no response. It made sense that an adult would have secrets they would want to keep from a child. Neither of them is even able to use the bathroom without the possibility the other may notice.

Flynae doesn't respond, but sadness overwhelms her as she tries to go back to sleep.

10

School (Flynae)

Flynae is putting her breakfast dishes in the sink when Eksar announces, "I want the both of you to get dressed and ready for school."

She and Sekara turn to him with furrowed brows, wondering what he could mean. Kaliah don't have any institutions similar to what humans call school. They are taught what they need to know within their family unit and are further encouraged to read and learn on their own.

"School, Father?" Sekara asks, her voice timid and hesitant. "Why?"

A heat spreads from Flynae's gut to her head. She fights to keep the anger from showing in her eyes. The control Eksar is exerting over Sekara infuriates her.

Flynae was surprised after their father's funeral when she heard Sekara called Eksar "Father" for the first time. When she asked her twin why, Sekara had confided to her that Eksar had told her to, and she was too afraid to disobey. The brief conversation had concluded with the twins holding each other and crying on the other's shoulders.

"Because Father has business today." He pets Sekara's hair.

Flynae's stomach twists and threatens to reject her breakfast. "We're just fine at home," she whispers.

His eyes narrow, and their color turns to show a hint of red. "You will do as you're told." He rises and stands over her.

She stands firm, her chin level, unwilling to be intimidated by him even as her small body betrays her by trembling.

"Now get downstairs and get ready."

Flynae walks steadily from the room though her instincts scream for her to run. *I will not give him the satisfaction of seeing my fear.* She breathes to control her emotions hoping that her scent does not give it away.

The basement is now a place of refuge. Eksar doesn't come down there often.

She goes into the little bathroom and stands in front of the mirror to braid the sides of her hair back from her face in a typical elven style.

After a few minutes, she is upstairs waiting with Sekara by the front door for instructions. Neither girl knows where they are going.

As Eksar approaches, the energy around Sekara shifts. A shimmer surrounding the dark-haired girl's head indicates that he has cast a temporary human disguise over her.

"Let's go," he says.

"What about me?" Flynae asks.

His narrowed eyes turn to her; she senses rather sees a smirk on his lips. "What about you?"

"Aren't you going to make me look human as well?" Her heart races. It is against all Kaliah protocol to not be disguised in human company.

"No. You may go just as you are."

Again, Flynae makes the conscious choice to not be afraid. She doesn't fear humans and has quite enjoyed interacting with the ones at the dance lessons she attended. Albeit, she was always disguised then. She squares her shoulders. "Okay."

Her confidence begins slipping as soon as they approach the human school. People of all ages stare at her. Children point; some laugh.

Eksar stops at the sidewalk, hands each of them a paper with directions and a schedule, and leaves.

Sekara and Flynae exchange a puzzled nervous glance and then walk inside hand in hand. Without any difficulty, they find the first classroom on the schedule. The twins take note of the names of each room they pass for reference later.

Inside the classroom are several little round tables with chairs, many already filled with children their age. The twins introduce themselves to the teacher at the desk and ask where they should sit.

"Anywhere you would like." Her eyes widen when she takes the time to notice Flynae.

The girls find two seats together away from the center of the room; the teacher follows them.

"Um, Flynae?"

Flynae respectfully looks up and meets her eyes.

The teacher shifts her weight. "We don't allow costumes in the classroom."

A few children close by snicker.

"Excuse me?" Flynae glances at her sister. Sekara shrugs; she is just as confused.

"Costumes are only allowed on Halloween."

"Understood."

The teacher still doesn't leave. Her weight shifts to her other hip. "I need you to remove yours."

"I'm sorry, I don't understand."

Impatience creeps into the teacher's voice. "Your ears." Her voice is strained, rising in pitch. "I need you to take off your ears."

Flynae furrows her forehead. A knot twists in her stomach. This is why she was supposed to be disguised. Eksar knew this would happen. "Take off my ears?"

The teacher huffs, obviously displeased. Her lips purse in mild anger. She reaches down, grasps the top of Flynae's ear, and sharply pulls.

As sudden as the teacher's movement was, Flynae's sharp reflexes see it coming. She swings her hand out wide and slaps the teacher's arm. Both of them pull away from the other. The teacher gasps and rubs her arm. Flynae puts a hand over her assaulted ear and scowls at the woman.

"You do not strike a teacher. You are coming with me to the principal's office right now." In a much louder voice, she says, "The rest of you stay in your chairs until I return."

All eyes are on the two of them as Flynae follows the woman from the room.

11

Intervention (Kovad)

Lord Kovad Thyde sits at his computer pouring over reports from his generals when he feels a tug on his left ear. Instantly, he is aware of where Flynae is and what has transpired in her morning that leads up to her being taken to the principal's office.

He sighs, closes his eyes for a moment to center himself, and then pulls up the number to the principal's office at the school. Now that he seemingly ruined this little girl's life, he feels a responsibility to help take care of her. A bigger picture lies behind the death of Issiah than Emperor Seko let on when he tasked Lord Thyde with exterminating him. He was never informed that Issiah was a Kaliah, much less of the Kaliah royal family.

How much difference would that information have made? Probably little. Lord Thyde would still have obeyed his liege. Would knowing more beforehand allow him to feel less dirty now? Absolutely not. He just despises being used as a pawn when he has earned his rank through years of faithful service and giving up everything else in his life.

Each question leads to another. Why is the Emperor interested in the Kaliah, much less the Kaliah royal family? Very few humans even know that the Kaliah exist.

And what is his plan for this little Kaliah maiden? Lord Thyde senses that she, too, is a pawn in a large scheme that he's only glimpsed pieces of. This furthers his resolve to keep an eye on her and intercede on her behalf when he can.

A pale male face pops up on the holocom. The man is sweating, having seen the identification of the caller before answering. "Principal Hillman's office. How may I help you, my lord?"

Lord Thyde needs no introduction. Every person in the galaxy knows his face. "Patch me through to the principal now."

The man nods and fumbles to remember to do as he has been told. "Yes, my lord."

Another nervous face appears before him. "L-l-l-lord T-t-thyde. T-t-to what do I uh uh owe the p-pleasure?"

Lord Thyde glances inside Flynae's head to see her present location in the school. The teacher has just left her with the flustered receptionist.

"A young girl is sitting outside your office. You will send her back to her classroom without correction and instruct your entire staff that they will make no comments ever concerning her physical appearance. They will treat her with the utmost respect at all times. Further, you will see to it that no one else on school property harasses her."

The principal's mouth hangs open. His eyes flick to the door to his office and back.

Lord Thyde is aware that Hillman has no clue about what he is referencing and doesn't care. The staff can fill him in on the details.

"Have I made myself clear?"

"Y-yes, my Lord."

"Good. I will know if anyone does not comply with this order.

Mr. Hillman gulps.

Lord Thyde ends the com and leans back in his chair to watch without drawing Flynae's attention to his presence in her mind. She is too distraught and distracted at the moment to notice him as she waits with trepidation on the bench. He admires her resolve to stay calm and keep her head up as she reminds herself that even though her father is gone, she is still a Kaliah royal and Issiah's daughter and will conduct herself as such.

A few moments later, Mr. Hillman emerges into the hallway. His eyes widen upon seeing Flynae. After collecting himself, he crouches down to her level. "What's your name?"

"Flynae Let."

"Let's get you back to your classroom, Miss Let. Okay?" He stands and reaches out his hand to her.

Flynae nods and gets up but rejects his hand, keeping her arms firmly at her sides.

When he begins walking, she follows him.

He opens the classroom door for her. "Go ahead and take your seat. Mrs. Meyers, I need you to step into the hallway."

Sekara whispers, "What's happening?"

Flynae mouths, "I don't know."

After a disapproving look at Flynae, the teacher joins the principal in the hallway. Even with the door shut, the twins can hear every word that is said.

"Why is she back in my classroom so quickly? She struck me."

"I don't care. I just received a com from Lord Thyde."

Fear, revulsion, and hate swirl in a nauseating circle in Flynae's stomach at the mention of her father's killer.

"He gave strict instructions that Flynae Let is to be treated with the deepest respect by everyone," the principal continues. "If anyone disobeys his orders, their job will be terminated immediately without severance. Do you understand?"

Apparently, Miss Meyers understood as she returned to her classroom without another word. Her demeanor was subdued, and she kept her eyes averted from Flynae as she continued the lesson for the day.

12

Freak (Flynae)

Flynae and Sekara found human school boring. They were being taught letters with the rest of the class while both girls were proficient in reading.

"Freak," the little boy across the table whispers to Flynae as she sits with her sister having lunch. The girls stuck close together and had been left alone by the students the first week. Now, the little humans were getting braver. The boy glances around and then turns back to Flynae. "You're a freak," he says a little more loudly.

Flynae regards him as much as she would a bothersome gnat flying around making its whining noises. The more she ignores him, though, the more persistent he becomes.

This time he leans forward across the table and says in a low shout, "Freak!"

Flynae would be amused if humans weren't quite so annoying with their requirement for acknowledgment. She understands enough now about humans in her one week at school that the boy needs her to react to his insults. He won't stop until she responds.

In her mind, she brings up the image of the human in black striking down her father. Instead of allowing herself to feel sorrow, she brings in all the hatred and rage she feels towards him until her hands tremble with the intensity of it.

She turns to Sekara and whispers, "Are my eyes red?"

Sekara leans back and smiles, wondering what her sister is about to do. "Very."

Flynae inclines her torso onto the table until her head is only a foot from the boy and turns her face to him. "Then why don't you go sit elsewhere."

The boy jumps back, all color draining from his face. Then he bolts from the table leaving his lunch behind.

As the twins share a giggle, Flynae allows the anger to release and dissipate. "That'll teach him."

A strong smell of ammonia reaches both of their noses making them crinkle.

"Ew," Sekara says.

"Humans." Flynae shakes her head. "They're so..." She looks around the room at the sea of them searching for the right word. "Useless? Delicate?"

"Delicate. Exactly."

Flynae sighs wishing that she could avoid the drama and come to school in a disguise like Sekara, but her energy control isn't strong enough yet. She's taken to clipping her claw-like nails short and wearing her hair pinned over her ears, but there is no covering up her eyes despite spending hours in a mirror practicing.

As Sekara and Flynae walk back to their classroom after lunch, three taller boys step into the hallway and stand in their way. Two of them are about eleven, and the third is probably thirteen. The twins move to walk around them, but their path is blocked.

One of the younger ones leans down into Flynae's face spitting on her as he says, "You're the freak that scared my little brother. He said you had weird eyes."

Flynae refuses to give an inch and doesn't react to the insulting moisture on her face.

"Bryan Aarndt," a teacher calls from behind the girls.

Bryan looks up, his face hardening, knowing he will be punished for even appearing to be rude to Flynae. "You're dead, freak," he whispers, and the boys move on.

Flynae and Sekara shake their heads. Flynae isn't worried. She knows she can outrun a human any day.

After school, the twins hug and go their separate ways. "Tell Senice I love him," Sekara begs.

"I will," Flynae assures her.

Eksar had enrolled Sekara in some afternoon classes at a local finishing school. Flynae had received no afternoon directions so far and had arrangements to meet Senice in the nearby park. She can barely contain her excitement as it has been ten days since seeing him at her father's funeral, and she misses him dreadfully.

Flynae hums as she walks towards the park. She's barely off school property when she hears Bryan Aarndt say, "There she is." The three boys are behind her, running in her direction.

"Oh gods," she swears under her breath and takes off. She'll either lose them in the city or lead them straight to Senice who will take care of them. At the moment they are just a nuisance.

The streets of Solum, the capital city of the planet Diomede, are busy as she runs through the downtown skyscrapers. Humans assume they rule this planet, like all the others, but it is actually under Kaliah control. The surface city is built on a mirage made of a permanent energy shield. Flynae can look down under her feet and see through it if she desires. Beneath it is the Kaliah "Underground", a flourishing city where Kaliah don't have to disguise themselves as no humans know of the Underground. Diomede is the control hub of the galaxy. Unbeknownst to humans, many Kaliah hold places of great importance in the human hierarchy of government.

A road in front of her is cordoned off from all traffic for a procession. After a glance behind her, she sees that she hasn't lost the boys yet. She darts down a side street to try to go around. After a few more turns, she finds herself lost and staring at a brick wall. She's in an alleyway that goes nowhere surrounded by buildings on three sides. Near the buildings are a couple of commercial trash compactors. If she stands on these, she might be able to jump and reach the bottom of a fire escape. While she contemplates her options, the boys come around the corner blocking her in.

Her eyes widen when she sees the oldest boy is holding a knife. "We've got you trapped now, freak."

13

Boys (Kovad)

Lord Thyde is acutely aware of Flynae's mild panic as she runs from the boys chasing her while he walks down the steps of the capitol building next to the Emperor. He sees the route she intends to take and knows that it is closed for the next few minutes until Emperor Seko is safely in his vehicle and on his way.

Seko seems to sense the distraction and turns and looks up at the tall human next to him. While the Emperor's presence is even stronger and more imposing than Lord Thyde's, the Emperor has a smaller, much more lean and elegant frame underneath his stately robes. He seems to float rather than walk as he moves.

"Something on your mind, Lord Thyde?" The Emperor's voice is as smooth as his gait, intoxicating and sultry to all who hear it.

"Just your safety, my liege," Lord Thyde lies, wishing the Emperor would hurry up and go. From the corner of his eye, he catches a glimpse of her long red hair turning down a side street. When his heartbeat quickens with her fear, he focuses on his breathing to remain calm and wait.

The Emperor studies Kovad for a moment and then glances towards where Flynae recently disappeared. Finally, Seko steps into his awaiting vehicle, and a guard closes the door behind him. Lord Thyde waits until it pulls away before walking swiftly after Flynae.

He delays until he is around the corner, out of view of the capital guards and the reporters that document the Emperor's every shit, before using energy to cloak himself and begin running. It would be scandalous for him to be seen hurrying. The cloak doesn't make him invisible, it just makes anyone around him not notice him.

After a couple of turns, when he has caught up and sees the boys at the entrance to the alleyway, he slows to his normal quick stride and allows the energy cloak to drift away. He feels Flynae's alarm at the sight of the knife in the boy's hand, but the sound of his footsteps distracts her.

She's back on the porch hearing his boots hit the ground as he walks toward her father. She begins trembling as dread fills her. His presence and proximity are more frightening to her than being cornered.

One of the boys turns, and his eyes widen when he sees Kovad. "Holy shit. It's Lord Thyde." They all turn toward Kovad and stand awkwardly, frozen by fear and awe.

Lord Thyde keeps his pace until he reaches the boy with the knife and picks him up by his shirt until their faces are only a foot apart. The knife falls from the boy's hand and urine drips from his shoe.

Kovad smells the urine faintly through his own senses while also noticing how strong it is through hers. He sees himself through her eyes and hears her pounding heart in her head.

In a calm, low voice, he says to the boy, "You let it be known to everyone at your school that she is not to be touched nor harmed by anyone. If she is, I will hold you personally responsible. Do you understand?"

When the boy nods and stammers, "Y-y-yes," Lord Thyde lowers him, releasing him a few inches from the ground to land with a jarring thud. As soon as the boy can collect himself, he races off with his minions trailing behind.

Kovad softens his face and demeanor and turns to Flynae, his countenance now one of remorse and sorrow. She is striving to channel her dread and horror into rage. Her eyes show a tint of redness.

He opens his mouth to speak, but she screams, "No!" before he can get a word out. She doesn't want to hear his voice and connect the one from her head to the man before her now.

She doesn't want his gesture of protection and would rather be fighting the boys to her death than facing him. With as much control and dignity as she can manage, she says, "Leave me alone. I don't ever want to see you again. Don't talk to me again. I want you out of my head." Her hands go to her hair and grip her scalp in a desperate gesture as if she could pull him out.

After considering and abandoning several things that he would have liked her to hear, he resumes his public demeanor, inclines his head towards her respectfully, and then strides back to the capitol building.

14

The Park (Flynae)

Flynae stands there with her heart echoing the thudding of his boots as he walks away. When the footfalls fade to just a phantom in her mind, she falls to her knees. How can *he* be the voice in her mind?

She'd trusted him, allowed him to soothe her to sleep. It feels like a betrayal to know the truth now. He purposefully hid it from her.

Her stomach swirls within her threatening to give up what little it contains. She breathes through nausea.

He'd intervened at the school as well. The knowledge comes to her mind as an unbidden memory from his.

Crush you. Leave me alone. I don't need you.

As the discomfort in her stomach diminishes, she struggles to blink back tears. She refuses to cry over him. He isn't worth it. Still, the tears swell up.

She feels lost and alone and shivers though it isn't cold out.

Senice. Flynae finally remembers what she was doing before the boys chased her. Nearly blind with tears, she races down the city side streets using only her instinct to guide her to her uncle. The skyscrapers give way to a park filled with sweet-smelling green grass and tall oak trees.

Her Uncle Senice is there, waiting for her on a bench. When he sees her, he realizes something is wrong and runs to meet her halfway.

"What is it, dear one?" He kneels in front of her, his hands gently holding her upper arms. After looking her over for damage, he surveys the landscape behind her. "Are you being chased?"

She shakes her head, not trusting her voice to get anything out between her ragged breaths. A single tear escapes down her cheek. She wipes the traitorous moisture away. After a deep sigh, she whispers, "No. Not anymore."

"Who was chasing you?" Senice's eyes narrow and sweep the view behind her one more time with a glare.

"They aren't important actually. I have something else to talk to you about."

He smooths her hair and kisses her forehead before rising, taking her hand, and leading her back to the bench where he sits patiently holding her hand until she is ready to proceed.

Her mind races, not knowing where to begin or how to form into words what she needs to know from him. Finally, her most pressing question surfaces in her mind. "How do you end a mindlink?"

Senice raises his eyebrows with curiosity. His head tilts as he looks at her. "That is quite the strange question, Flynae. What does that have to do with the panic that you flew into the park with?"

More tears find their way to the surface of her eyes. She tries to blink them back feeling ashamed at her lack of control. "Because." Her voice catches in her throat. She swallows hard.

"I think I'm mindlinked with someone."

"Really? Who?"

The lack of judgment in her uncle's voice gives her the courage to continue, but she can't bear to say his name. Her head falls forward. "The man who killed my father."

"Kovad Thyde?" Senice doesn't hide his surprise and soothingly strokes her hand.

She nods.

Senice pulls her into his lap. Flynae leans against his shoulder enjoying the warmth of his body, the security of his arms about her, and the soft, steady beating of his heart.

"I want him out of my head, Uncle Senice." Her voice hitches a little as she tries not to cry. "How do I get him out?"

"I take it this just happened last week?"

She's grateful that he didn't give words to the horrible act that started it all. "Yes."

"You never said and I guess I never asked what fully transpired that day. Did Lord Thyde touch you? I didn't know the two of you got that close."

"Right after he—struck down.... I ran out. Even though Father said to stay where I was, hidden out of view. I couldn't. I ran out thinking I could stop him from dying. Then *he* grabbed my arm. I think he was going to kill me, too. At that moment, I saw him while seeing myself through his eyes. I didn't understand until today who the voice in my head belonged to."

Senice takes a deep breath and thinks for a moment. "Wait. What happened today?"

Flynae relays the events of the morning and finishes by saying, "When I saw myself again through his eyes, I realized who I had been talking to at night." A shudder runs through her small frame.

Senice listens patiently until she gets everything out and stops.

"Eksar sent you to school without a disguise?" The words come out with a low sound like a growl in his throat.

"Yes. He disguised Sekara, but not me."

Senice's arms tighten around her; she can smell the sharp bitter smell of his anger. He waits until his heartbeat and breathing are almost back to normal before speaking again. "All right, I'm going to meet you outside school on Monday mornings and disguise you. It'll hold for most of the week. You'll need to learn how to strengthen it so that it lasts. If I ever can't meet you, I'll try to let you know. On those occasions, you'll need to wear some contacts to hide your eyes, which I'll get for you, and wear your hair pinned down over your ears or a headband to hide your ears. Okay?"

"I can do that." Flynae waits patiently for Senice to address her main issue. Finally, she can't keep her peace any longer. "But what do I do about *him*?"

Senice sighs. "I don't have great news for you there, dear one. I have never heard of a mindlink being broken except for one of the beings linked dying."

Flynae swallows the urge to yell out, "Then let's kill him." She has been taught to regard all life as precious.

"What have you two talked about?"

"Meditating mostly." With some reluctance, Flynae shares with him that Lord Thyde has been kind to her whenever the two of them converse. "He's helped me go to sleep most nights." Her mind wars within her wanting to keep separate the kind voice in her head from the image of the human who cut down her father.

"He's not a malicious human by nature, dear one. I might

call him a little misguided, but not malicious."

"You know him." She looks up at her uncle, her brow furrowed and her lips pursed.

"Yes. Though it has been several years and promotions since I've seen him."

Flynae stops seeing through her eyes as she turns her attention inside her mind. "He's listening right now. We often know when the other is thinking about us." Her face twists as she concentrates to sense him without being invasive or engaging. "I think he respects you, Uncle. How do you know each other?"

"When he was in a relationship with the daughter of a dear friend of mine, I helped him to improve his energy control and his lifesword skills. I took you to see the daughter once when you were an infant. Your father found out I took you near a human and was livid." Senice laughs.

"Shame on you," she says with a smile. "You know how Father feels about them."

"He made it abundantly clear."

Flynae evaluates the emotions flooding into her mind that aren't hers. "Why does talking about–?" she searches for the name that is in *his* mind, "Cellyna. That's her name. Why does she make him–?" The emotion is convoluted and layered. She guesses how to describe the gist of it. "Sad? That's the closest word I know for it."

"Well. They were married until he left her. I don't know his reasons, because I know that when he left he still loved her."

"He was trying to protect her," Flynae says, repeating what she heard in *his* mind without thinking. Then she grabs the sides of her head with her hands. She doesn't want to understand him as a person. If she does, then she might not be able to keep hating him. If he isn't all bad, then she won't be able to hold onto her anger towards him.

"Hey now." Senice lovingly brings her arms down and squeezes her. "I love you, dear one. I will do everything I can in my power to protect you, but I don't know how to help you with this except for being here for you when you need to talk about it."

Senice holds her until she has regained some calmness and composure. "All right. We need to do some practicing." He sets her on her feet and holds out his hand in front of her. Energy swirls above his palm in a soft shimmering circle. "This is the energy I use to disguise myself. Touch it. Feel it."

Flynae's eyes widen with desire. She longs to harness and manipulate energy as easily as her uncle does. She reaches out her hand and places it in the middle of the energy ball feeling it electrify her skin. It's soft and warm and playful. She closes her eyes allowing her energy to dance with it.

"Yours will be a little different when you can do it on your own, but the core of the feeling will be the same. Understand?"

She nods, keeping her focus on the glowing air.

"I'm going to bring it to your face. Allow it to flow through your skin. Support and contribute to it." She puts her hand by her side as his moves towards her. When it is close, the ball floats to her and becomes one with her. She knows without seeing that she looks like a human without a trace of Kaliah traits to give her away.

"Relax when you work with it. You can't force it to do what you want. Think of it like the way you dance and play with music in the air. It is no different."

15

Why (Flynae)

Flynae spends the day feeling conflicted about Lord Thyde. Her uncle seems to think of him without animosity, and she trusts Senice implicitly.

Now and then the energy on her face distracts her. She tries to play with it and contribute to it without diminishing it.

As afternoon fades to evening, she knows that she must head home. Home is too warm a word for the way the place makes her feel. She loves her sister, but being around Eksar every day is unbearable. He looks at her with disdain all the time. She wishes she knew why he hates her so much. The air is difficult to breathe when they are in the same room.

As she dissects the smell he gives off when he's around her, she realizes it isn't hate. It's something much thicker and often makes her skin crawl. She doesn't have a word for it.

Flynae is surprised to see three places set for dinner each night. She's prepared for Eksar to refuse to let her eat with them. She's shocked that they eat dinner together at all. No one says much. Even Sekara who he dotes upon is nervous around him.

Flynae stabs a piece of raw steak with her fork. As she raises the bite to her mouth the cream walls and dark wooden furniture of the dining room fade from her vision. Instead, she sees the pale skin of a man's bare back.

She feels as if her left arm draws back and strikes a leather whip against the white skin leaving an angry red welt that oozes blood in spots. The man gasps.

Everything happens in slow motion.

The left arm lifts again and lays another wound across the first. The man howls in an awful cry of pain.

She drops her fork and holds her hands over her eyes hoping this will block the sight as she begins screaming, "No! No! No!"

The left arm rises again and halts. She feels turmoil, a mental battle of whether to continue or not. A trickle of crimson traces its way down the man's back to settle into the waistband of his pants.

As the left arm lowers with the lash in hand, the right hand comes up to rub *his* face in frustration. She hears him inhale deeply and exhale slowly.

"Stop. Please," Flynae begs forgetting where she is and only seeing the horror in front of *his* eyes. She's jarred back to reality by someone grabbing her hair and pulling her from her chair.

Sekara stares at her as Flynae is yanked backward across the room.

The whip is passed to another hand. "Continue," *he* says as he walks from the grey room to an equally grey hallway.

Flynae feels the impact of each stair as the acquaintance between them and her hip grows. Eksar doesn't slow until she is in the middle of her room where he leaves her and slams the door behind him.

Flynae holds her hands to her face and sobs wishing she could forget the red lines on the man's back. The image is forever burned in her memory. His wail replays in her ears.

Minutes later, she begins to come to her senses and realize that Kovad Thyde has been sitting on the edge of his bed waiting for her to regain her composure.

Apologies, he says when she notices him. *I'm not used to needing to consider you when I do things. If I had, I would have waited until you were asleep.*

What kind of apology is this? she thinks exasperatedly only realizing after his sigh that he has heard her. *Why would you do that at all?* She can't hide the scorn in her thoughts.

She has a front-row seat to him running through his possible answers. He finds worth in his skill in being able to "break" people and get what he wants from them. This is when he feels the most in control. Being in control is important because he doesn't trust/approve of Emperor Seko. He knows that thought is treasonous.

She sees in his mind a blurred image of women walking around and dancing on a stage wearing nothing more than string bikinis while the Emperor and his lords watch. Some of them are too young to be called women. From the back of the room, one of them screams. She feels his cheeks burn with rage and helplessness. Being powerless is his most hated feeling.

Flynae sits down on her bed and listens/watches his train of thoughts, shuddering at the last image.

Fuck. I can't think about anything without you seeing. I didn't mean for you to see or hear all of that.

His conflicting emotions bring her discomfort, especially after talking to Senice about him in the park. She doesn't want to see him as *human*. He's the monster who murdered her father in front of her.

To distract herself and distance herself from him, she looks down at her legs beneath the hem of her skirt. She's bruised from hip to ankle. Walking tomorrow is going to be painful. And she'll need to wear long pants to school.

I'm going to sleep now. She feels as if it would be rude not to tell him since they had recently been conversing. She slowly lifts her legs onto the bed and lays down.

16

Halaa (Flynae)

"Senice is picking you both up after school today," Eksar tells the twins over breakfast.

Flynae does her best to remain composed and not show her excitement. She's found that it's better not to let Eksar see her emotions. Her eyes remain focused on the bowl of fruit and cup of raw egg in front of her.

"Where is he taking us?" Sekara asks. She's beginning to learn that Eksar doesn't get angry with her, and she can pretty much do whatever she wants.

"That's a good question." Eksar's eyes narrow. "It'd better not be someplace that makes me angry. I don't want to completely cut him out of your lives." He turns his gaze on Flynae. "At least at this point."

Flynae swallows hard and resists the urge to look up and examine his face. *He's baiting me.*

"Where will you be?" Sekara asks.

Eksar reaches out and strokes her cheek making Flynae's stomach clench and hurt. "I have important business away this week."

Sekara takes a sip of her egg. When she does, Flynae notices her stomach turns. Then she realizes that it was not her stomach. *He* had noticed their breakfast and was working to control his natural reaction to it.

Flynae can't help but frown. *I don't understand what is so gross.* She looks down at the berries, melon, and two raw eggs in front of her and sees food that would be delicious were it not being consumed in Eksar's presence.

Your eating habits are not gross to me. I just prefer to eat my egg whites cooked is all.

Flynae wrinkles her nose. *Now that sounds unappetizing.* Like all other Kaliah, Flynae can't think of meat that she would prefer cooked. Whether it is mammal, fowl, or reptile, she likes her protein raw.

She glances around the room looking for something to distract herself with. The strong emotions she had recently felt because of Eksar's words had attracted his attention. She's not ready and doesn't know if she will ever be ready to have a casual conversation with him again.

***

"Senice," the twins call out in unison as they run out of school and see their uncle and their brother waiting for them. They both stop short of colliding with him and wait for him to place his hands on their temples and kiss their foreheads in typical Kaliah greeting. Flynae is first because she is the elder by a few minutes. When she turns to Fennec, he hugs her instead.

"Who have you been hanging out with?" she asks surprised at his lack of decorum.

"I know. Bad manners," Fennec says with a smile. "It just becomes habit so easily."

"Where are we going, Uncle Senice?" Sekara asks.

"To Halaa," he replies with a quick mischievous lift of his eyebrows. "I have a friend I want you both to meet."

"Cellyna," Flynae says without hesitation.

Senice inclines his head. "You are very astute, dear one."

"Who's Cellyna?" Sekara asks her sister as they follow Senice to his shuttle.

"A human."

"Eww." Sekara rolls her eyes and throws her head back dramatically. "I've had enough of humans at school lately."

"I think you'll find her agreeable," Senice tells them. "And if you don't, then at least you girls can learn to ride a horse."

Flynae's breath catches in her throat from excitement.

"Yes, please," the twins say in perfect unison.

The flight to Halaa takes four hours. The planet lies in a less populated corner of the galaxy where the planets are either mostly wild or used for farming. As they descend, Flynae notices that there are no major cities in view, just small villages or single farmsteads dotting the green countryside. It's a lush green and brilliant blue planet covered in fields, forests, and plenty of bodies of water.

The shuttle comes to a landing in a clearing across from an old-style ranch house that Flynae has only seen the likes of in books. The bottom floor has a wrap-around porch while every room on the second level boasts its own balcony. Several stone chimneys stick up from the roof.

Close to the house is a massive barn with a footprint three or four times that of the house. White wooden fencing connects to the barn and goes on for as far as one can see. On the other side of the house across from the barn is a large open-air arena.

A human stands waiting for them on the porch. She's slightly taller than average height for a human female with a slender yet strong build. She wears clothes that the twins have only seen in books or on television: cowboy boots, blue jeans, and a pink and black plaid button-up. Her long auburn hair is pulled into a low pony over her shoulder.

When Senice has turned the shuttle engine off, he instructs the twins before they disembark. "I just want to warn you that Kaliah children are especially irresistible to humans. She will probably fawn over you all weekend. Please be polite and respectful. She really can't help herself."

The twins exchange a look and a groan before reassuring their uncle that they will remember their manners.

As the four Kaliah walk to the house, the human's eyes widen and her face lights up as she gets a good look at the twins.

"Oh my god, Senice, they're adorable."

Flynae is surprised when her uncle embraces the human who is only about two inches shorter than him and kisses her cheek. When the human wraps Fennec up in a hug, Flynae realizes where he'd acquired his habit of embracing beings.

When Senice and Fennec stand aside, Cellyna kneels in front of the twins so that her face is nearly level with theirs. "I'm Cellyna. You probably don't remember me 'cause you were both babies when you were here last, but I certainly didn't forget either of you. Let me see if I remember. Flynae has the red hair, and Sekara the black?"

The twins nod in confirmation.

Flynae inhales and notes by her scent that the human is excited. She also smells something that leads her to think the human has a romantic attachment to her uncle. Flynae feels a little bit of sorrow for her. While Senice may care for her and call her his friend, Flynae has heard him express his intention to never have another intimate relationship with a mortal.

"I have some food set out on the back deck," Cellyna says as she stands and leads them through the house.

Flynae can tell by the selection of food before them that the human knows what Kaliah prefer to eat. There are plenty of raw nuts and meats and fresh vegetables and berries. Maybe this visit won't be so bad after all.

17

Emotions (Flynae)

After a busy day of riding horses, collecting eggs, milking a cow, bottle-feeding baby goats, picking berries, and chopping wood, Flynae is exhausted but unable to sleep. She's surprised by the endless number of things to do on a farm.

She and Sekara were given a shared room and bed. Her sister had fallen asleep quickly with her arms around Flynae's neck. Her breathing is low and peaceful.

After laying there for at least thirty minutes with sleep being no closer, Flynae slowly and carefully wriggles out from her sister's embrace and tiptoes silently from the room.

A light shines through a partially open doorway at the end of the hallway. She hears canned laughter from a show.

Flynae walks down the hallway past doors on either side towards the light. She can tell which rooms Senice and Fennec sleep in by their scent even though neither of them has gone to bed yet.

She peers into the room where the noise and light are coming from and sees Cellyna sitting against the headboard of a big oak wood bed watching television.

Cellyna glances in her direction. "What the fuck?" she shrieks, nearly falling off the bed in her fright.

Flynae takes a couple of steps backward, her heart racing, wondering if she has done something wrong.

"No, wait," Cellyna calls out. "I'm sorry. Come in."

After a moment's hesitation, Flynae steps into the doorway.

Cellyna's chest rises and falls with deep breaths as she works to calm herself. "You can come in, Flynae. The eyeshine still catches me off guard when I'm not expecting it."

Flynae nods to make the human feel better but still doesn't understand what is so shocking about eyeshine. Kaliah eyes have a layer of tapetum lucidum just like any cat does that reflects light and makes their eyes appear to glow.

"Can't sleep?" Cellyna asks, pausing her show.

"No." She shakes her head. There's been too much change in her life and sleeping quarters lately and a general lack of feeling secure. Settling down for the night has been difficult. Especially since she hasn't been wanting Kovad's help relaxing.

"Want to come watch a show with me for a bit?" She pats the bed next to her.

Flynae considers and can't think of a reason not to at least join her for a little while. There aren't many other options that she knows about to do this late at night.

"What are you watching?" Flynae climbs onto the bed and sits down maintaining some space between her and the human.

"It's called a sitcom. It's supposed to be funny."

Flynae watched for a full episode and didn't find the show to be funny. The characters often made silly mistakes and put each other down a lot. It was beyond her knowing as to why humans would watch it or think it was humorous.

As the show lost what little interest it initially held for her, Flynae began taking in the room. On the nightstand next to her was a picture of Cellyna wrapped in Kovad's arms. They were both several years younger and appeared to be happy in the photo.

When Flynae turns away, she notices Cellyna watching her; the human's eyes are now sad and her scent has changed.

"Do you miss him?"

The human's emotions come pouring out of her like a tidal wave that washes over Flynae and causes her to feel the grief and pain she now smells.

"I do."

They sit there in silence for a few moments until Cellyna turns the TV back on. The emotions don't wane. Finally, Flynae can't bear them anymore.

"I think I'm sleepy now," she lies. "I'm going back to bed."

"Okay. Sweet dreams."

Flynae walks silently from the room and down the hallway carrying the human's emotions as well as her own confused feelings. As she reaches her bedroom door, Fennec comes out from his.

"What are you doing up, Fly Girl?" he asks softly, sensing her mood.

"I couldn't sleep. So I watched a show with Cellyna."

Fennec glances down the hallway towards the human's room and exhales. "Uh-huh." He turns back to Flynae. "Come with me. I want to show you something."

Flynae follows her brother through his room and out to the balcony. Spaced apart where each bedroom ends and the next begins are waist-high dividers, giving each room its own semi-private porch. Fennec lifts her onto one of these and gracefully jumps up behind her. Then he sets her onto the roof and effortlessly ascends himself.

They lay back and look at the stars together, their heads gently touching. Flynae marvels at the brightness of the stars when they aren't competing with nearby city lights.

She finds herself thinking about Kovad. Because of her recent interaction with Cellyna, she feels both the human's emotions towards him and her own: missing him and hating him at the same time.

"You've got to be careful around humans, little sister. They use Kaliah as a form of – therapy, I guess is the best word – when they're around us. They don't mean to, but they pass their emotions on to us. I don't think they even realize what is happening. In their minds, our presence just provides them with relief. Until you learn how to protect yourself, you shouldn't get too close."

Flynae relaxes into her brother's calm, even presence. At some point, she drifts off. She's barely aware when he lifts her and carries her back to bed.

18

End of Part One (Flynae)

"Flynae, would you run upstairs and tell Cellyna breakfast is ready?"

Flynae sits at the table with her sister watching Senice and Fennec prepare a morning meal that will appeal to both humans and Kaliah.

Without making a sound, she runs up the stairs and down the hall. Cellyna's bedroom door is open at the end of the hallway, and Flynae wonders if the human ever actually closes it.

"Cellyna," she calls out peeking her head around the door not wanting to surprise the human like she did last night.

"I'm in here," Cellyna hollers back, her voice coming through her open bathroom door.

Warily, Flynae walks through the room to stand in the next doorway.

The human has one foot on the floor and one foot on the sink and wears nothing but a cami and panties.

Flynae's forehead furrows in confusion. "What are you–?" She quickly turns away aware that if she attracts Kovad Thyde's attention he will see the woman in her current state of undress.

"I'm sorry."

"You're fine, Flynae. What's up?"

Flynae glances at the human out of the corner of her eye momentarily forgetting why she came upstairs. Cellyna is running a small metal wand up her leg over and over.

"Shaving." Cellyna laughs. "It's something adults do."

"Adult humans, you mean."

"Are you saying Kaliah don't remove any body hair?"

Flynae considers the question. "What body hair?"

"Like hair on their legs? Or armpits?" Cellyna switches which leg she's standing on and proceeds to use the wand and same motion on her other leg.

"Kaliah don't have hair on their bodies."

Cellyna stops and stares at her with wide, incredulous eyes. "Are you telling me that when you get older, you'll only have the hair on you that I can see now?"

"Yes. Just the hair on my head, my eyebrows, and my eyelashes."

"You don't have any peach fuzz on your arms and legs?"

"Last I checked, I'm not a peach so no, no fuzz." She stifles her amusement sensing that the human is entirely serious in her line of questioning.

"Show me."

Flynae walks forward and offers up her arm for the human's inspection. She fights her instinct to jerk her arm back when Cellyna takes it and runs her hand up and down her arm. Then the human brings her face close to it and looks at it from several angles.

"That is just silky smooth skin. I have to admit, I'm a little jealous."

Flynae steps back when her arm is released.

Cellyna muses for a moment and then asks, "What about the men? Do they have more hair than the women?"

"No." Flynae shakes her head to give more weight to her answer.

Cellyna huffs.

"Senice said to tell you breakfast is ready." She turns and heads out the door.

"I'll be down in a minute," Cellyna calls after her.

* * *

After they've participated in the morning chores, the twins are given some time to wander and do whatever they would like. After hours outside in the fresh air, they meander back into the house to look for a snack.

Piano music from one end of the house draws Flynae's attention. The quality of the sound indicates that it isn't being played by someone with a lot of talent, but it is still pleasant to the ear.

After following the sound, Flynae happens upon Cellyna in a room at the far end of the house sitting behind a baby grand piano.

Two of the walls in this room are mostly windows with a set of French doors leading outside. The afternoon sun is just beginning to gleam through the top of the windows filling the room with a warm light.

Flynae has never seen a piano in person before though she knows what it is from pictures. It's an instrument that a human is more likely to own than a Kaliah.

Cellyna smiles at her when she enters. Flynae knows the human has taken a liking to her. The Kaliah has much more mixed emotions towards the human. Still, she trusts her uncle's judgment that there are worse things in the galaxy than fraternizing with humans.

Flynae steps into a ray of sunlight and listens to the music, allowing its vibration to caress her body. Beautiful music feels like the presence of an intimate, almost sensual friend to her.

Sekara joins them shortly bringing with her a snack of cheese and berries which she shares with her sister.

They both listen until Cellyna stops playing.

"May I try?" Flynae asks as the human stands up.

"Sure. Have you ever played before?"

"No." Flynae slides onto the bench where the human was sitting. "But I watched you." Starting at one end, she presses each key a single time listening to how it sounds until she has traveled down the entire thing. Then she begins pressing a few keys at a time until she begins playing chords. Within a minute or two, she flawlessly duplicates one of the songs Cellyna had recently played.

The human's mouth drops open. "Wait. I thought you said you'd never played before."

Flynae looks up at her inquisitively wondering if there was a question she had missed. "I haven't. This is the first time I've touched a piano."

"Then how-?" Her eyebrows lift dramatically.

"When you know what sound each key makes, it's easy to put them together."

* * *

Leaving Halaa was difficult for the twins. They'd enjoyed interacting with the animals, being around Senice and Fennec, and sharing a bedroom again. In the end, they both had a slight affinity for Cellyna.

It was most painful for Flynae to leave the light, free feeling of the planet behind and return to the stifling, dungeon of her basement.

She did find something to look forward to each day when Senice surprised her by enrolling her in dance classes after school. In no time at all, she learned and grew tired of ballet, jazz, and ballroom. When she tried figure skating at the age of six, she knew she'd found one that she could happily do for the rest of her life. She also met Will.

19

Dress (Flynae)

When Flynae wakes up on the morning of her twelfth birthday, she is surprised and perplexed to find a pinup rockabilly halter dress hanging on the inside of her door. The straps and waistband are black while the main fabric is an emerald green that matches her eyes. She recoils at the thought that Eksar had hung it there while she slept.

The garment is beautiful, but she eyes it warily. Eksar has never bought her a gift before. What could be his motives for doing so now?

The material is silky about her body, but she's tense as she steps into it, her stomach clenching into painful knots. She isn't sure whether or not she has a choice to wear it. How would Eksar respond if she came to breakfast wearing something else? Flynae admits to herself that she is too afraid to find out.

At least once a week, he finds some reason to slap, punch, or bruise her in some manner. Several times, he has pushed her down the stairs.

Flynae covers her bruises and tells no one about them. Senice always looks at her as if he suspects something, and he asks all the time if she is doing well, but he is the last person she will voluntarily tell about the abuse. The tension between Senice and Eksar continues to grow. She won't add to it.

The only one who truly knows the extent of what she has endured is Lord Kovad Thyde. Their relationship has grown from her trying to tolerate him to an almost friendship. Whenever she is hurting and feeling alone, his presence is comforting and soothing.

Flynae fastens the straps of the dress around her neck and heads to her little basement bathroom mirror to do her hair. A large purple bruise stands out on her upper arm. With a sigh, she pulls in some energy from around her and provides herself with a suitable cover-up for it.

Her skill in energy work and manipulating her appearance is improving, but hiding the bruise and keeping it hidden leaves her needing to disguise her eyes and ears in other ways. Senice won't be on the planet today to help.

She brushes her hair over her ears and holds the tips of her ears in place with a silver circlet headband. Then she places the contacts over her eyes.

Satisfied that she looks as humanoid as she is capable of, she heads to the stairs. At the bottom of them, she stops for a moment, her body trembling in fright. A stabbing pain throbs in her lower gut. Her hands wrap around her stomach as she bends forward at her hips.

She concentrates on deep breaths, and the pain fades away. It wasn't real but was most likely a premonition. She's been having more of them as she gets older, flashes of things that will shortly come to pass.

She can't delay any longer though. Eksar will be angry if she is late for breakfast.

Flynae discovers Sekara in a dress of the same style but yellow to match her twin's eyes.

"Oh," Sekara calls out at the sight of her sister. "Aren't the dresses beautiful!" She twirls, allowing the skirt to flow out around her.

Flynae graces her sister with a smile. "Yes, dear one."

Eksar has done his best to put a wedge in the girls' relationship. They no longer attend the same classes and barely see each other. Some of it has worked. Sekara hangs out with her preppy crowd while Flynae spends her free time at the ice rink with Will.

Flynae takes her place at the table. Normally, Eksar pays Flynae little attention when he is around her, but today she feels his eyes crawling over her bare arms and shoulders like a cluster of ants she can't wipe off. She retracts her energy inside herself wishing she could slip away or become invisible. Anything would be better than sitting in front of him now.

His smell is strange, too. It's dark and musty and thick. She dissects it while wishing she couldn't smell it. Her palms begin to sweat.

Power. Lust. Desire. Control. She searches for the correct word to describe what she is smelling. The more she examines it, the more uneasy she feels.

Lechery. Lord Thyde adds his thought to her list. His mind voice is full of displeasure and controlled rage.

A cold shiver runs down her spine. His word is most apt for what she is smelling. What does this forebode?

Flynae hurries through her breakfast eager to leave the table and escape Eksar's leering gaze.

As the girls walk to school, Sekara notices her sister's discomfort. "What's wrong?"

"I don't know." Flynae is scared and confused but has no way to express that to her sister. Sekara has grown to be fond of Eksar over the years. He has doted over her and seems to genuinely care about her as well. Flynae doesn't want to express unfounded ideas.

20

Their Place (Flynae)

Dinner and the rest of the evening at home pass without incident. Flynae begins to relax as she heads down the stairs for the night wondering what had gotten her all worked up and remembering how huge Will's eyes had gotten when he saw her in the dress.

There had been more than a touch of desire in his scent today which made her feel bad. Will was her best friend; but as she got older, the more he began to take notice of her in other ways. She didn't know how to head off the inevitable situation of him eventually asking her out, and there was no way she was getting in a relationship with a human. Still, she didn't want to hurt his feelings.

She gets ready for bed and meditates until she falls asleep.

A swoop of cold air wakes her as the blankets are pulled off. A firm hand covers her mouth.

Her eyes fly open, and she can make out the face of Eksar above hers, his eyes narrowed with lust and loathing.

"Don't you dare scream," he whispers coldly.

Her heart begins pounding wildly against her ribcage. She

pushes against his hand as she struggles to get enough air through her nose.

His other hand reaches down to grab the waistband of her night pants, his claws scratching her skin open in the process. She barely registers it in her panic.

The fabric tears, making a horrible ripping sound.

Flynae beats against his arm which painfully holds her head down with much of his weight. She kicks her legs about, trying to find some way to get leverage.

Moments later, she finds herself naked from the waist down. She struggles to breathe. Her pulse pounds in her head. She's horrified and helpless as Eksar begins to unbuckle his pants.

Her mind shifts briefly as Kovad Thyde stirs in his sleep. Her terror is directing his attention to her. She has a moment to notice that she doesn't want him to wake and witness what is going to happen. A tear escapes and slides down her temple as much as she doesn't want Eksar to see her cry.

A dark, smooth metal ceiling appears above, much different from the rough concrete one she sleeps under, and realizes Kovad's eyes have opened. He's barely awake for a second before he understands what is happening and feels her horror.

Then, her awareness is first pulled and then gracefully swept away to the in-between, to "their place" as she often calls it. Their place is a state of consciousness where their minds are no longer separate but become one like the edges of a circle overlapping.

They had first found or created it when meditating together. It can look like any landscape they want it to, but it often looks like a meadow because of her desire to be surrounded by nature constantly.

It is night in the meadow, and the display of thousands of

stars in the sky above them captures her attention. She shivers, and he wraps his cloak around her. Her body jerks, but he gently stops her from turning her head to look back through her physical eyes at what is happening.

Just be here with me, he whispers.

She leans against him knowing that he stands between her and her awareness of something awful transpiring.

Lord Thyde's arms pull her to him. His body twitches with controlled rage. He lifts her and sits down on the grass, holding her close, and takes a deep breath.

She feels his overlying anger and underneath a heavy weight of guilt. She lifts her gaze to his and sees his eyes and her own, glowing with the reflection of soft starlight, at the same time. The corners of her mouth lift in a slight smile. *Meditate with me?*

His eyes slowly close. *Always.*

***

When Flynae returns to cognizant of her body, it's because she is violently shivering. The first thing she remembers is being with Kovad in their place. Her cheeks flush as she recalls letting him hold her. That was a first, and she wonders what overcame her that she would allow him to get that close.

The dull pain in her groin and lower abdomen hits her next. She rolls to her side and draws her legs up trying to ease it as she fights the wave of nausea the pain brings. The metallic scent of blood irritates her nostrils. Her blood.

The room is pitch black.

She reaches for her blanket, and her torso is tickled by threads of fabric. Upon inspection, she finds the front of her camisole is shredded. The skin of her torso is scratched and warm to the touch.

She can't find a covering on the bed and drops to the floor to search. Finally, her fingers happen upon the blanket. She pulls it around herself, aware that she is getting blood on it, but she needs to feel covered.

Flynae crawls across the floor, towards the light switch. Every moment is agony. Her legs are bruised. She feels Eksar's hands pushing her legs apart. Hot tears burn their way down her cheeks.

Keep moving, she tells herself, not wanting to be stuck crying on the cold cement floor.

Finally, she finds the light switch and turns it on. When she turns and sees the blood on her bed, her stomach threatens to empty up what little contents it holds. It isn't the sight of the blood that bothers her, it is the memory of what caused it that her body carries.

She forces herself to stand on her shaky legs and strip the sheets from the mattress. While clutching the blanket around her shoulders, she carries her linens to the laundry and starts them washing. Then she heads to the bathroom.

A shower sounds like too much effort. She turns on the bathwater, climbs in, and sits down as soon as there is a little warm water covering the bottom of the tub. She sits there shivering, hugging her knees as the water rises slowly around her.

While she would rather not think of anything at all, her mind can't stop going back to what she remembers. Eksar's hand presses against her mouth again and again. Acrid tears stream down her face.

When she looks down at her body, deep purple bruises stand out from the light skin of her chest, her stomach, and her inner thighs. The bathtub water turns a slight shade of pink as the blood is washed from her lower half.

She's too numb to fully weep.

Her mind begins to consider the day ahead of her. How is she going to sit at the breakfast table across from Eksar? What can she say when Sekara asks what is wrong?

As she sits there in anguish, she's distracted from herself as she notices Lord Thyde waking. He must have fallen asleep while meditating with her.

Don't look at me, please. She averts her eyes from her body knowing that he can see whatever she does through them. She's painfully aware of her nakedness.

He searches his mind for something to say.

There's nothing to say, she tells him.

21

Ice (Flynae)

Flynae doesn't know how she survived sitting at the breakfast table the next morning except that her heart refused to quit beating. Eksar sat across from her with a smirk on his face noticing the long sleeves and pants she wore. Her stomach wouldn't even allow her to look at food as it churned within her threatening to spill up bile.

When Sekara asked what was going on as they walked to school together, Flynae had no words for her sister. She just shook her head and kept walking.

After school, she rushed to the ice rink.

Will was waiting for her. He's three years her elder and almost a foot taller than her with a lean, muscular body and dark skin. Whenever she looks at their hands together when he holds hers, she thinks that if someone made a statue of the two of them, it would be called "marble and ebony".

The stark contrast of their skin tones adds to the beauty when they dance together. His black hair sits on top of his head in tight little curls kept neatly short.

When he sees her that day, his eyes narrow and his brow

furrows. They've been dance partners for nearly five years, and he can read her emotions almost as well as if he could smell them.

As she walks up the few concrete steps, Will asks, "Flynae, are you okay?"

She doesn't know how to answer his question, so she just keeps walking as he holds the door open for her.

"Thanks," she mumbles as she passes him.

"Flynae," Will calls out as she heads towards the locker rooms.

"I just want to get on the ice," she replies without slowing. Once she is there, she sits in a quiet corner, puts her head in her hands, and begins to shake. She's had these moments all day long during any period of silence and inactivity. The night before comes back to her: Eksar's hand on her mouth, her gasping to get enough air, her body jerking as it is violated. She feels it all as if it is happening again, right in front of anyone around her.

Are you sure this is a good idea today? Once more, as he has been all day when she's struggled the most, Lord Thyde is there.

I have to continue as if nothing has happened. No one can know.

Why don't you tell Senice?

If he tries to confront Eksar, he'll die. I can't lose him, too. The image of Senice standing up to Eksar morphs into her father being struck down by Lord Thyde. She falls to her knees, stifling the cries in her throat. There are too many humans near for her to be able to weep.

A locker door slamming brings her back to the present. She stands up and tries to compose herself, determined to be brave and carry on. She slips off her pants and feels them being ripped from her. Her hands shake as she undresses and pulls on her practice clothes.

Will is waiting for her just outside of the girl's locker room. She takes a wide path around him, bumping her shoulder into the wall as she avoids getting close to him.

"You can't hide that something's wrong." He follows her to the corner where they typically warm up with some active stretches. Kaliah don't need to stretch the way that humans do, but the movement feels good, and she always tries to mimic human behavior when she's around them.

She sighs and looks up into his concerned deep, brown eyes. "I'm not trying to hide it so much as I'm trying not to think about it. I definitely don't want to talk about it." Her words come out a little more harshly than she would like, but it's too late to take them back.

"Okay." He holds up his hands in surrender. "But if you want to talk to someone, you know I'll always listen, right?"

"Yes." She manages a small smile for him, knowing he deserves that much from her. "Thanks, Will."

They finish stretching in silence and then head out onto the ice. The sound of the blades on the ice relaxes her. She closes her eyes and listens, her other senses able to alert her to glide around people and not run into sidewalls.

"Shh. Everything will be alright. Shh," the sound of the ice purrs in her ears. "Shh. You're safe here. Shh."

She wraps her arms around herself as she shivers in the embrace of the reverberations across her skin. It's like gentle fingers that caress and release the tension from her muscles. Almost instantly, she feels calmer.

They skate apart for a little while, practicing little jumps and edges. A dozen other people are at the rink practicing as well. As is usual, they all find themselves a bit distracted when Flynae takes the ice. Humans tend to become mesmerized by Kaliah, even hypnotized to an extent. The effect is amplified by the Kaliah's age and focus.

When Flynae opens her eyes, she finds that everyone else has stopped and is watching her. She'd forgotten anyone else was there as she listened to the song of the ice.

She blushes and retracts her energy, releasing them from their trances. One by one, they shake their heads and remember what they were doing. Their focus on her when she is alone makes her nervous. Somehow it is always better when Will is with her, holding her hand or her waist.

Will comes to her now, his hand extended. She touches it and then recoils, her body remembering another scene from last night when Eksar pressed her hand down against the bed.

"Flynae? It's just me." H e frowns with worry.

Flynae swallows hard and holds up a single finger turning away from him, fighting the tears that threaten to spill. She smells his hurt and concern and is sorry to be the cause. She listens to the ice again.

"Shh. You're here in your safe place. Shh. You can be strong here. Shh."

After a few deep breaths, she returns to Will, skating backward in front of him. "Okay. Let's do this." She tries to smile for him, but it falls flat.

His face scrunches in skepticism, but they begin to try a few basic maneuvers together. After some synchronized footwork and spins, he comes in for a lift. His hand goes to her waist, and her whole body tenses up. She feels Eksar clawing at her torso, and her skin burns beneath the touch.

Will tosses her into the air, and she teeters a little on the landing as she struggles to maintain her balance. The whites of his eyes stand out in his dark face from surprise. He's never seen her come close to losing her balance.

"Oops." She gives him a small grin to diffuse the tension. The feeling was a little unnerving for her as well. She's used to being able to rely on her natural cat-like grace as a Kaliah.

"Are you sure this is a good idea?"

"There's nothing else I'd rather be doing." Flynae knows she would be losing it even more if she wasn't skating right now. "Maybe just give me a little more alone time?"

"Whatever you want." Will sighs and skates away.

Flynae knows that she is continuing to hurt his feelings, but she can't do anything about it today. She's barely holding herself together. All that she is capable of right now is getting lost listening to the ice beneath her skates.

"Shh. It's just you and me. Shh."

After a while, she looks around and sees Will sitting on the sidelines watching her. The rest of the rink is empty.

"What-?" She skates over to him, pursing her lips in puzzlement. "Where-?" She motions at the empty rink.

"Everyone went home, Flynae. It's been a few hours."

"Oh." She glances up at the clock before looking back to Will. It's late, but she doesn't care. She doesn't know how to drag herself back home. Her throat tightens thinking of Eksar's face over hers, his eyes staring down at her in menacing delight. "Is it too late to practice our routine?" They are hardly ever here late enough for the ice to be empty. From his smell, Will is more worried about her than anything else.

Will raises an eyebrow but then goes and puts on their music.

Flynae's stomach knots when she takes his hand to assume their starting pose. She wants to pull away and shrink back into nothing. Instead, she forces herself to remain calm and breathe through the instinctual panic.

When the music begins, her movements flow and become one with his. The ice whispers to her; the music caresses and relaxes her.

They skate apart for a synchronized spin and then come back together. His hand finds her waist. Her calm disappears as alarm grips her.

Focus on the music, she tells herself. *It's just Will.* But her body feels Eksar over and over again.

Suddenly, a hand on her inner leg lifts her in the air, but she feels Eksar pushing her thighs apart. She's back in her bedroom struggling against him.

Will screams her name.

* * *

Stunned and confused, Flynae blinks her eyes. When she turns her head, the pain is immense and throbbing.

Will is on his knees next to her, looking down at her.

"What? Where am I?" She tries to sit up, but he holds her down.

"Will, no," she screams in terror and thrashes.

"Flynae, please don't move. You hurt your head. Please stop moving."

The look on his face confirms that his concern is real. She inhales and smells his shock. This is enough for her to relax on the cold surface.

"It's bleeding so much. I need to stop the flow and then go call for help." He slips off his shirt and pushes her headband out of the way. He stops and stares at her head for a moment with wide-eyed wonderment. "What the-"

She realizes he is staring at one of her tall, pointed ears. Her hand instinctively moves to cover it.

"Don't be daft." He brushes her hand out of the way. "I've got to slow the bleeding."

The hand that touched the side of her head is covered in blood. She stares at the crimson liquid, shuddering as she sees the blood from her legs running off into the bathwater the previous night.

Are you all right? Lord Thyde's urgent question conveys his concern.

"I don't know. That's a lot of blood."

"What don't you know?" Will asks. "Yes, it's a lot of blood."

She looks up at Will's face and finds it dull and ashen. "Does the sight of blood bother you? You look a little ill."

He nods. "This much blood bothers me. Yeah."

She winces as he tightens the fabric against her head.

"I think I got it." Will slowly pulls his hands away.

Help is on the way, Flynae. Stay as you are.

Thank you. Despite the ice beneath her, Lord Thyde's reassurance warms her.

"I'm going to call for help." Will moves to stand, but she grabs his hand. "Flynae, let me go. I have to get you some help."

"Help is on the way."

"How? There is no one else here. Are you delusional?"

"Help me get off the ice, please." The cold is becoming unbearable.

"You shouldn't move. What if you broke your neck or back?"

She turns her head side to side. The motion makes her dizzy, but she doesn't feel any serious pain from her neck down.

"Nope. Don't think anything except my head is broken." Her body begins trembling from shock or the cold of the ice. "I'm freezing though. I'll die of hypothermia before the paramedics arrive if you leave me here. Help me up." She rolls to her side to try to stand on her own.

From the corner of her eyes, she notices Will looking around like he's evaluating other options before he turns back to her. "Wait. Don't move. I got you." He kneels and scoops her into his arms as gently as possible and carries her from the ice. "Now where-?" He stands there like he's unsure of what to do with her now.

The motion makes the room spin. She focuses on breathing to keep nausea at bay. "Just sit with me."

"Flynae, I have to call for medics." The pitch of his voice rises with his increasing panic.

"Trust me, Will. They're on their way." She touches his face with her fingers and pushes some calming energy his way. "Now sit down, please. You're making me dizzy. I don't want to throw up on you."

"Don't die on me, Flynae." He clutches her to him, sits down on the ground, and holds her close.

Two minutes, Lord Thyde says with certainty.

"Two minutes, Will." The room is fading around her. "Please. Just. Wait...with...me."

22

Hospital (Kovad)

When he enters the hospital, the intensity of experiencing her senses heightens. He smells the highly alkaline, sterile smell of bleach. He hears the consistent, irritating beeping of the heart rate monitor connected to her. It chirps along at sixty-five beats a minute. She notes that it is a little fast for her normal rate but understandable in her current condition.

When he gets off the elevator at the floor she's on, her delicate ears pick up the steady pace of his boots echoing through the empty halls. Her heartbeat quickens. It's the same steps she heard when he came to kill her father.

Lord Thyde adjusts his gate, setting his feet down more gingerly. His tactic works. The sound isn't quite the same, and she relaxes to her former state.

He reaches the door to her room and pauses with his hand on the handle wondering if he should have come. He is here for selfish reasons, wanting to see with his own eyes that she is all right. It's too late to turn back. She's looking at the door, waiting for him. He presses the handle down, his own heart beating a little faster.

As he enters, he sees the large form of his frame filling most of the doorway while also seeing the outline of her body on the bed and her eyes, two halos shining around the contacts meant to disguise them.

Flynae's initial reaction is to close her eyes, hiding their uncommon glow. The resulting darkness is stifling and causes her to tense.

You don't have to hide them from me.

His voice in her head is soothing. She recognizes it as a friend.

You don't have to hide anything from me.

After a sigh, she opens them and looks at him again.

A heaviness settles into his chest. It's a mixture of his emotions and hers. He knows she's in a great deal of pain from the cut on her head and the resulting surgery but doesn't understand why. He feels her fear of and desire for his presence. He acknowledges the royalty and beauty before him and finds himself lacking.

Flynae reaches out her hand.

His heart swells like it would break from the confines of his chest. He hasn't allowed himself to care this much about someone in more than a decade. He won't allow her offer to go unanswered and quickly crosses the room to take her hand.

"Mmm. Your hand is so warm." Her voice is barely above a whisper.

Her spoken words are like a beautiful melody to his ears. As intimate as their thoughts are, he finds himself longing to hear her speak more aloud.

She shivers.

"You're cold?"

"You'd think they were storing bodies in here, not living beings." She offers a smile with her humor, and he can't help but think she is the most beautiful thing he has ever seen.

"I can find you another blanket." He glances around, ready to storm out to the nurse's station and demand several more immediately.

"That would require me releasing your hand." Her grip tightens. He is her lifeline, her hold on sanity. Despite his initial faults at the beginning of their relationship, he has become her friend and protector, her safety. "Would you sit next to me?" She wants to feel physically secure the way that he makes her feel mentally protected.

She scoots over as he sits down on the bed; her face twists in a grimace she can't hide.

"Why are you in so much pain? Do you need more analgesics?"

"No." The word comes out more aggressively than she intended. After a moment to get her breath back, she explains further in a calm voice. "The human ones aren't strong enough for Kaliah."

"What do you use then?"

"Kya leaf. It's like a cross between a poppy, belladonna, and cannabis plant, only much stronger."

"Does it make you high?" he asks with a chuckle.

"In certain doses, yes." The pain has dulled again as she remains still, and she becomes aware of his body so close to hers on the bed.

"I can find a chair."

"That's not necessary. You smell good."

"I should hope so. I showered today."

She closes her eyes while smiling at his joke, knowing that he fully understood her meaning. Her smile turns into a grimace as she recalls everything that has led them to this point: him killing her father in front of her, him almost killing her as well, him trying to protect the child whose guardian he annihilated, him trying to fulfill that guardian role as best as he could. Even if from a great distance.

Flynae closes her eyes against the tears that well up and leans her head against his shoulder.

Why did you come here tonight? She knows her voice will break if she speaks.

I needed to see that you were okay.

Is this considered okay?

No. But I will take from you what I can and shelter you from the rest.

He begins an energy pull from her, transferring as much of the pain from her head to him as he is able.

What are you doing? She yawns. As the pain lifts, fatigue quickly sets in.

Helping you rest.

But you'll be gone when I wake up. Her eyes close as she begins to relax.

I never fully leave you.

She sleeps.

23

Hospital (Flynae)

Flynae wakes up when the door to her hospital room opens. She felt more refreshed than she had expected. The pain and pressure in her head come back quickly though.

Her body shivers with cold, and she longingly remembers feeling *his* heat next to her. The visit was unexpected and pleasant. She didn't realize how much the mindlink had made her long for his physical presence.

The nurse starts, and her eyes widen as she comes around the curtain and sees Flynae.

Flynae remembers, having seen herself through Kovad's eyes last night, that her ears are standing out quite prominently over the bandages wrapping her head. Thankfully, she was wearing her contacts when she got hurt. At least she didn't have two abnormalities for them to stare at. She wonders how much hair she is missing from them stitching her back together.

On the chest of the nurse's bright yellow scrubs is a name tag that says Shahedyn.

"Oh, you're awake already. I was just coming to check your vitals." She moves to the computer monitors and inspects them. "How are you feeling?"

Flynae closes her eyes with a grimace as she thinks and evaluates her answer. "Like my head is about to explode," she replies in a low voice.

"Hmm. Your records say that you are receiving a regular dose of opioids every four hours. If you feel like you need a little more, you have a button here you can press."

She acknowledges the device though she knows she won't use it. Human painkillers make her feel strange, a little out of her senses.

"You shouldn't be in pain. I'm a little surprised you're awake already."

Flynae politely nods and sighs, feeling as if the nurse is just talking to herself at this point.

The nurse turns from the monitor and looks at Flynae, being very mindful of maintaining eye contact. "Do you need anything right now?"

"No, thank you."

"Well, we're just a push of a button away if you change your mind." Shahedyn leaves her in peace.

With nothing to drown out the noises, Flynae hears everything going on in the hospital around her: the beeping of many monitors, sneakers scuffling on linoleum floors, nurses chatting at their stations. She turns on the television and finds a music channel to give herself something else to focus on.

A couple of hours later, someone brings her a tray of breakfast. The smell of the food alone makes her stomach flip as she stares at scrambled eggs that must have come from a bag, limp bacon, and white toast with butter and jam on the side.

Her first thought was, “Do I have to eat this?”, and after a taste of the eggs, she knew it wasn’t going to happen. The smell of the processed bacon was too overwhelming for her senses in her current condition. She took the water off the tray and pushed the rest as far away as she could.

When Flynae heard someone approaching her room next, she wondered if she was going to be scolded for not eating. Instead, the nurse brought a second tray.

“Someone called in a special meal for you,” the nurse explains as she used the new tray to push the first one off into her other hand and then rolled the stand it was on to within Flynae’s reach with her foot.

Flynae now finds before her a plate of fresh fruit and a small cup with two raw eggs. A warm tingle runs through her. She knows who ordered this. Her body breaks out in goosebumps. *Thank you.*

You’re welcome. I hope you are well enough to eat.

The pain in her head makes her stomach quite upset, but she manages to get down some of the fruit and then close her eyes for a bit. Resting is difficult as she can’t keep herself focused on the music. She keeps feeling a hand over her mouth or holding her down or forcing her legs apart whenever she closes her eyes.

Approaching footsteps pull her out of her dozing daymare. Two women enter. One is the nurse Shahedyn from earlier. The other is wearing black slacks and a white button-down blouse.

“Hi, Flynae,” the business-looking woman says, pronouncing her name correctly with a soft “i” sound. “My name is Sandi Coll. I work in Human Services here at the hospital.” She sits down in the chair close to the bed while the nurse hovers around the foot.

A lump grows in Flynae's throat. She knows what this is about. The lady should take a hint from the tall, pointy ears she is trying not to stare at and recognize that this is not a human issue nor is it one that any human can solve. She struggles to keep her hands relaxed as she vacillates between shame and rage.

"I wanted to talk to you about some bruises and marks the doctor noticed that were inconsistent with the head trauma you suffered at the ice rink yesterday."

Flynae's cheeks flush, and she swallows with difficulty.

"Has someone been violent or abusive to you recently?" Sandi Coll asks.

Flynae refuses to break eye contact or make any indication under her conscious control to give credence to the allegation. She takes a breath and says calmly, "No."

The woman's shoulders drop. "Flynae. We can help you if you'll talk to me. We can protect you and make sure it doesn't happen again."

It takes all her self-control not to laugh. There is no one, and especially not these humans before her, who can protect her from Eksar, except for maybe Siah, her father's oldest son. A new monarch must be recognized at some point, but Siah might not even know that their father is dead and that the Kaliah need him.

The social worker sighs. "Alright then. If you don't want to talk about it, I can't make you; but I do hope that you will talk to someone before you are released. If you change your mind, let one of the nurses know." The two women leave together.

Her headache is worse after the discussion. She leans back and focuses on her breath, hoping to find a sliver of relief.

Flynae doesn't hear the arrival of her next visitors as they make no sound as they walk. She turns her head when she hears the door creak open and is delighted to see Senice and Fennec entering the room.

"By the gods, what are you doing here?" She sits up too quickly and is rewarded by a stabbing pain in her head. She grimaces and clutches the side of her head.

The look on their faces is one of serious concern. Fennec rushes to sit next to her and gently puts his arms around her.

Senice walks around the bed and kisses her forehead before sitting down near her.

"How did you know where I was?"

"I received a comm from Lord Thyde."

She closes her eyes and thanks him for the second time that day.

"And," Senice pulls a drawstring leather pouch out of his pocket, "he said you needed this."

She can smell the kya leaf inside and eagerly holds out her hands. Her uncle gives her the pouch, and she pops a pinch of it in her mouth and chews it a little before holding it there to be absorbed into her bloodstream. The taste is intensely bitter, but she knows she will feel better in a few minutes. As the pain in her head begins to dull and ebb, she drifts off into a deep sleep.

24

Discharged (Flynae)

Senice and Fennec stay with her that night in the hospital. The staff tried to insist that only one person was allowed to stay, but Senice was adamant that neither of them was leaving. He slept on a cot that was brought in while Fennec slept next to his sister and held her all night. She had no nightmares.

When Senice asked her what had happened, Flynae only told him of the accident on the ice. He'd narrowed his eyes at her response, knowing she wasn't telling the whole story but didn't press her to share more than she was willing to.

The three of them are eating a lovely breakfast Senice ordered for them when Eksar strides nonchalantly into the room. He takes a moment to examine their faces each in turn. When his eyes fall on Flynae, she wishes the floor would open up and swallow her. The hint of a grin appears on his face. Flynae's spine feels encased in ice.

She notices Senice bristling, but he does that anytime he's around Eksar. She isn't sure if he noticed the look or not. At least he doesn't know the meaning behind it.

At that moment, both Shahedyn and Sandi Coll enter the room. The nurse holds a chart and the social worker holds a clipboard.

"Looks like you're ready to go home," the nurse says with a note of concern. "The doctor has agreed to an early release since your guardian said you'll have constant supervision."

Flynae realizes that Eksar had arrived to hurry things along.

Sandi looks at Flynae and raises her eyebrows. "As long as you are ready to be released."

Flynae realizes the woman is trying to give her a way out, one last chance to talk to her. There is no way she can say anything in front of Eksar and her family. Who knows what Senice would do if he found out. She won't risk it.

Having only missed half a beat, Flynae says confidently, "Of course I am."

Sandi exhales sharply through her nose. "All right. Everyone out so she can get dressed." As the door closes behind them, she whispers, "This is your last chance if you want to say something."

Flynae's hands shake slightly as she puts her shirt on. It would be naive to think that Eksar wouldn't violate her again. The question is when?

Sandi touches her arm. "It's not too late, my dear."

"I'm just a little light-headed from standing." Flynae adds a forced laugh. "I'm not used to being upright yet." Her pain is minimal thanks to the kya leaf. Nothing compares to the dread of going home. Once she is dressed, she follows the nurse out into the hallway. The nurse tries to offer her a wheelchair ride, but she refuses.

Flynae takes Fennec's arm for balance and keeps her chin up. Her external facade is strong and proud. Inside, she tries to think of whatever she can to avoid sinking to the floor and sobbing. *I am my father's daughter.* Her eyes remain dry.

The tears threaten again when they're outside, and it's time to say goodbye to Senice and Fennec. They both gently touch the sides of her head and kiss her forehead. She grips them each tightly in a hug, and they squeeze her lovingly.

Then she steps back and manages a convincing smile before turning and walking with Eksar to his shuttle. Her stomach grips her guts in horrible knots at the thought of being alone with him.

He just smirks at her and then ignores her for the rest of the trip. They arrive home before Sekara is out of school. When Eksar heads to his office, Flynae gets a book from their extensive library and finds a remote spot outside to read.

Sekara finds her sister when she gets home from school. At her sister's prodding for information, Flynae shares only what happened at the ice rink. The girls hang outside until it's time to go in for dinner.

Flynae is barely able to eat and blames it on her head when Sekara asks about it. The truth is that Eksar's presence has her insides all twisted.

Flynae lies awake listening for hours after going to bed, but the night passes without incident.

25

Kaliah (Flynae)

The damage to her hair wasn't intolerable. She'd hit her head right below her hairline so not much of it had to be shaved away. A loose-fitting headband covered her ears and the bandages.

After school, she makes her way to the ice rink out of habit and desire. The ice was the only place she felt in control of anything.

Since she takes longer than usual to walk from school to the rink, Will is already out on the ice when she arrives. He smiles and comes skating over as soon as he notices her.

"Hey. What are you doing here?" His grin fades, and he narrows his eyes at her, showing that he is clearly suspicious of her intentions.

"What do you mean? Where else would I be?" She doesn't have hope that she can just shrug it off, but her options are to pretend everything is normal or to completely melt down. Her body trembles as she struggles to hold herself together. She walks towards the locker rooms.

Will follows. "You don't intend to skate today, do you?"

She keeps her head high, her voice steady. "Of course, I do. Why else would I be here?"

Will exits the ice, puts on the blade guards, and hurries to block her path. In his skates, he looms over her more than usual. His hands move to take her by her shoulders, but she steps back just out of reach and looks up at him.

"Flynae, you just suffered a traumatic head injury." He shudders. "I'm still traumatized from it myself. No doctor would clear you for physical activity yet. I'm surprised you're out of the hospital and up walking around.

She holds her ground and stares at him, maintaining a look of defiance so as not to give in to the threatening tears.

"Hey." He steps a little closer.

She doesn't move.

He leans down and wraps her in a hug. It's the first time they've been close in a way that wasn't related to their skating practice.

She stiffens. It's too dangerous to relax. The dam holding back her emotions is tenuous. Her body is too exhausted to hold all the tension she carries. Something small gives and she leans into him. His arms squeeze her tightly. A rogue tear slips down her cheek. She doesn't beat herself up for it because he didn't actually see it. The comfort feels good. She needs it.

After she takes a deep inhale and lets it out, he releases her and stands up straight again. She can smell and sense him working to control his emotions and hormones.

"I've got an idea." He holds up his hand in a waiting motion. "Let me go get changed. Don't go anywhere."

When she gives the slightest of nods, he darts away as quickly as he can on his skates over the thin carpeting to the boys' locker rooms.

Flynae rests against the wall and closes her eyes. The sound of the other skaters on the ice calls to her. She wants to be out there.

A sense of relief floods her, and she recognizes that it isn't her own. Lord Thyde had been watching, full of nervousness that she was going to skate today and impede her recovery.

Will comes back in his street clothes wearing jeans and a black t-shirt under a black leather jacket walking with a touch of swagger.

Flynae stifles a laugh with a hand over her mouth. He's always wearing clothes like this off the ice.

"What?"

"What are you?" she teases with a smile, "some sort of biker?"

Will takes her hand and continues his swagger as he pulls her along with him. In the parking lot behind the rink is a motorbike. It's nothing fancy or huge, but she can tell that it has been given lots of love and attention. It shines in the sunlight.

Will doesn't release her hand until they're next to the bike. He casually throws a leg over and straddles it. Then his eyes meet hers with a piercing look that makes her insides tighten.

"Are you an elf?"

Flynae's mouth drops open. Her eyes widen. "What?" She wishes she'd heard him wrong.

"I saw your ears when you hit your head." His voice is casual, conversational.

Her hands fly up to the sides of her head as if her ears were visible now.

"Don't be embarrassed." One side of his lips lifts.

She manages to close her mouth, and slowly brings her hands

down.

"Well?" he asks again, "are you an elf?"

A lump asserts itself in her throat. She can't believe she's having this conversation with a human. He is different from the little boy who had called her a freak on her first day of school though.

"No. I'm not an elf," she replies with a twinge of sadness. To most Kaliah, the differences between the elves and the Kaliah are astronomical. Elves are perfect. The Kaliah are tainted, perverted, less than. Her eyes shift down and away.

"Then what are you?"

For a brief moment, she feigns innocence. "What makes you think that I'm not human?"

He tilts his head and drops his chin in a "come on, quit teasing" look. When she hesitates, he says. "Just look at you. You're perfect. Strong. Fast. Like superhuman. You hear a song once, and you have it memorized. Our choreographer gives us our routine once, and you know it inside and out, never making a mistake." His forehead crinkles. "And you're gorgeous. I've never seen anyone as breath-taking as you."

Her only defense is to deflect. "That's some mighty high flattery, Will."

He shrugs his shoulders. "So?"

She doesn't want to be having this conversation. It's not something she is supposed to discuss with a human. She doesn't want to hurt his feelings either. "Was this the only place you were planning on taking me? Out back to the parking lot to interrogate me?"

"It's not. But I'm not moving until you tell me."

She turns away, crossing her arms, stomping her foot in frustration. Why won't he let this go?

"If you don't tell me," he teases, "then I'll just call you an elf."

This is the remark that hurts deep in her being. He doesn't understand that she would never even pretend to be an elf. Tears threaten, and she struggles to speak through the vice grip on her throat. She turns back to him with pleading eyes. "Please don't."

His grin immediately fades. "Woah. I didn't know it would make you that upset." He begins to stand.

"No, don't." She holds out her palm towards him to coax him back down.

He slowly sits. "I didn't mean to distress you."

"I know." She has herself mostly under control again. "But you can't call me an elf."

"Why not?"

Because of the softness of his voice and the concern in his eyes, she decides that maybe it wouldn't be the worst thing in the galaxy to let him know. After a shuddering breath, she begins, "I'm a...." She had to break eye contact to find the words. "Cursed. Mutated elf." Her eyes come back to his. "I'm a Kaliah."

Will stares at her entranced, soaking up her every word, her every movement. "What's a Kaliah?" he breathes.

"Four millennia ago a sorcerer somehow combined night stalkers and elves. The result was a race similar to elves, but physically faster, stronger, more resilient. He kept them as slaves and made them work in his mines."

"So Kaliah are way cooler than elves," Will says with a knowing nod.

"No." She frowns. "We're tainted. Defective."

He eyes her up and down. "You don't look defective to me."

She huffs, slightly annoyed that he isn't hearing her. She holds up a single finger in a "wait" motion and turns around to take out her contacts. Then she turns back holding her breath as she lets Will see her eyes. She studies his face for his reaction.

At first, his eyes narrow as he tries to focus and comprehend what he's seeing. Then they widen as he leans back a little. His mouth opens before any sound comes out and forms a huge grin. "That's so cool." He stands up from his bike. "May I look closer?"

Involuntarily, she takes a step back, surprised by his reaction and feeling vulnerable and exposed. "I guess."

He leans down, putting his hands above his knees until his face is level with hers and just a foot from it. "They're like a cat's. Is that what a night stalker is? A cat?"

"Yeah," she whispers uncomfortable with his face so close, but she is determined to hold her ground. "They're similar to a, uh, big black panther."

He moves his head slowly from side to side, peering into her eyes from every angle.

"Can you see in the dark?"

She blinks slowly and then holds his gaze again. "Yes. As long as there is just a tiny bit of light from the stars or the moon."

"Okay," he says abruptly, standing up to his full height again. "How is this a defect?"

"Well, I, um, have pronounced canine teeth when I am angry or think about–meat." She opens her mouth as her fangs elongate. Before he can respond, she closes it and holds out her hands. "I have to keep my nails trimmed short or they become like really sharp claws."

Will crosses his arms, leans back, and looks down his nose at her. "So in other words, you are telling me that you are some sort of insanely cool vampire cat elf?"

Flynae stares at him, not knowing what to say. She's been taught that Kaliah are inferior to elves. The elves are perfect; the Kaliah are tainted.

I'm going to have to agree with Will on this one, Lord Thyde thinks casually.

By the gods, you're always listening, she replies with feigned exasperation.

Only when it's interesting.

Her head is spinning as she tries to examine this new way of looking at herself. "I guess." She doesn't sound convinced and turns to put her contacts back in.

"Wait. Why are you doing that?" He puts his hand on her arm to stop her.

"Because I can't go anywhere without them." She looks up at him earnestly. "And you can't tell anyone about me. Understand. No one."

He balks and shifts his weight a little.

"Will," she says sternly.

"Okay." He makes a motion of running a zipper across his mouth.

"Thank you. Now, where are we going?"

"Oh yeah." He sits back on his bike. "Climb on. I'm taking you to my house. There is something there I think you'll really enjoy."

She gingerly sits down behind him and places her hands on the sides of his waist. Without another word, he starts the bike and drives away.

26

The Band (Flynae)

"This is your house?" she asks as she climbs off the back of Will's bike.

She follows him as he rolls his bike through the gate next to a simple two-story tan and light blue house with a small, manicured front yard in a suburban area on the other side of town from where she lives.

"This is it." In the backyard is a small shed where he parks his bike, sets the combination lock on the door, and gives it a little tug.

From the other side of the house coming from inside the garage, she hears music: drums, a keyboard, a guitar, and someone male singing.

"What's going on inside?" The music is practiced and sits in that limbo above amateur and below professional. Like all music she hears, it calls to her.

"My brother's band practice." He takes her hand and leads her up the steps to the deck, through a sliding glass door, and into the kitchen.

The smell of baking bread welcomes her. She inhales deeply.

Flynae sees his mother standing at the counter looking at a cookbook, surrounded by a sea of vegetables, and her cheeks flush, understanding the connotation of Will holding her hand. She's familiar with his family, having seen them when they would drop Will off for practice or attend one of their junior skating competitions.

"Good afternoon, Mrs. McNeal."

"Flynae. Good to see you. How is your head?" She glances at their linked hands.

Flynae inwardly groans, but she won't embarrass Will by extricating herself from his grasp while his mother is watching. It isn't insupportable. "It is healing quite nicely. Will is providing me with a distraction to keep me from the ice today."

Mrs. McNeal nods with approval. "As he well should. It is much too soon after your accident for you to skate, my dear."

Flynae closes her eyes and bows her head slightly in acknowledgment.

"I thought Flynae might like to listen to Ryen and his band practice."

"That's a lovely idea, son." She kisses first his cheek and then Flynae's. "Are you kids hungry?"

Will begins to pull Flynae again as he moves through the kitchen to the garage. "Starving."

Flynae restrains her chuckle to a quick exhale. Will is a bottomless pit when it comes to food.

His mother glances at Flynae.

"I'm just fine, thank you."

Mrs. McNeal frowns. "Girl, you are skin and bones. I'll have some snacks together in no time, and you'd better eat some."

"Yes, ma'am."

Will pulls her through the garage doorway, and the door

swings shut behind them. The music washes over them like a wave of welcoming energy.

Flynae grins, enjoying it already. She recognizes Will's brother Ryen standing at the lead mic with an electric guitar in his arms. The two brothers' physique and stature are as different as their vocation. Will has fifty pounds of solid muscle on his older brother and stands three inches taller.

Will points to the drummer and yells into her ear, "That's Dusty." He points to the keyboardist, who also has a mic and is singing backup vocals. "That's Kris."

Flynae reclaims her hand as they sit against the wall on a bench near a teenage girl who is maybe a year or two older than Will. "This is Carmi," Will introduces them. "Ryen's girlfriend. Carmi, this is Flynae."

"I remember you, Carmi. You were with the family last month at the competition we won."

"Yes," she squeals. "You two were magnificent. Breathtaking. There was no doubt in my mind that you were going to take first."

The three of them turn their focus back to the band and listen. The quality of the music and singing has subtly increased since Flynae and Will arrived. Flynae notices and knows it is because of her. Kaliah lift and influence humans with their presence.

After a couple of songs, the guys take a break. A table in the corner of the garage waits with sweet tea and numerous finger foods provided by Mrs. McNeal.

Carmi jumps up clapping. "That was inspired!" She squeals and wraps her arms around Ryen's neck.

"It felt pretty good," he admits. He glances at Flynae with a welcoming smile. "Will is bringing in groupies for us, I see."

Introductions are made with the other two band members.

Flynae makes sure that she is referred to as Will's skating partner.

Dusty gives Will a wink, saying, "Riiight."

"Do you play?" Kris asks her.

"I'm familiar with the piano."

"Want to play us something?" Ryen asks.

"I would love to. It has been a while." She observes as Kris changes the keyboard setting to piano and then perches on the bench. She decides on a haunting pop-rock song that they've probably all memorized and begins to play and sing. After just a few notes, jaws drop. Carmi's eyes mist up; by the end, she is silently weeping.

When Flynae stops, there is a moment of silence as everyone needs time to recover from the exquisite, painful beauty of her music.

Ryen turns to Kris. "You're fired. We've got a new keyboardist."

Everyone laughs, needing relief from the unexpected poignant emotions.

Flynae's cheeks grow warm. She smiles and shakes her head. "I would never."

"Yeah, but seriously, we should get a second keyboard so you can play with us," Ryen continues with a teasing grin at his younger brother. "No more ice skating for you."

Everyone laughs except Will. Flynae smells and senses his possessiveness of her even before he speaks and takes a slight step toward her.

"Hey, I didn't bring her here so you can steal her into your little band."

"Calm down, baby brother." He thumps Will on his back before turning to Flynae. "You're welcome to come back and hang out any time."

A mixture of warmth and reservation wars within her. She's just made several human friends. Her father must be "rolling in his grave" as humans say. "Thank you. That's very kind."

27

Asked (Flynae)

Two years later…

"How about this one?" Will hands one of his Bluetooth earbuds to Flynae.

She slips it into her ear and listens. The song has a strong, catchy beat that makes her want to tap her foot and shake her hips. The lyrics are a little dirty, typical of the music Will enjoys. She allows herself to feel the music and move with it. It's definitely something she can dance to. Still, it's good to maintain the upper hand.

"I'll consider it." She hands the device back to him.

He grins as he takes it. "You like it."

"I never said that." She focuses on retrieving the books for her next class from her locker. At the end of the school a year and a half ago, Flynae enlisted Senice's help to transfer to the school Will attends. Sekara wasn't one to be left behind and transferred as well.

As Flynae pulls the book she needs from the compartment in front of her, the metal door slams shut with a bang. She blinks and groans.

"Seeing as how we are the two most attractive people in this joint, it's only fitting that we go to the dance together."

To her right, Eric leans against the locker next to hers looking his version of cool and casual. His hair is slick with gel and pulled back from his forehead. His cheap cologne burns her sensitive nose. He's dressed, as always, in the latest preppy style.

She looks at Will and rolls her eyes, knowing he shares her feelings about this smarmy character. "Did you really just call yourself attractive?" She turns and walks away from him as she tries not to smell any more of his toilet water, arrogance, and lust.

"So what if I did?" Eric trots to get ahead of her and stops her in the middle of the hallway. A lock of greasy hair falls into his face; he runs his hand over it to put it back into place. "I know where I stand."

"Really? Cause if you did, you would know you're right in my way." She ducks to the side to get around him.

He reaches out to painfully grab her arm just above the elbow. "Are you turning me down?"

She meets his eyes without flinching or blinking, annoyed with his superiority.

His nostrils flare in surprise and anger. "You'd better think hard about your answer, Flynae. There are ramifications for turning me down."

She smells Will's indecision in wanting to defend her without overstepping boundaries. She's told him many times that she can look out for herself.

Wanting to play a little with Eric, she puts on her innocent, pouty face, the one that makes humans like Eric weak in the knees. Her eyes, which she can now have appear human on her own, grow large as she tilts her chin down. Her lips purse. She stands on her tiptoes to whisper in his ear, smelling his desire for her growing stronger as she leans closer. "I'm turning you down."

With a simple flick, her arm pops free of his grasp, and she walks down the hallway knowing he is left standing with his mouth agape.

Will rushes to catch up and fall in step next to her. "So. It sounds like you aren't going to the dance with Eric."

She laughs. "What gave you that impression?"

"Let's call it a keen sense of intellect."

"I would call you correct."

"Well, about the dance-."

When he pauses for air, she interjects a question for distraction, " Did you ask Lycelle to go with you?"

Lycelle is a sweet girl who has a huge crush on Will. Flynae has heard him mention more than once that he thinks she's attractive. Flynae hopes to direct his attention toward a human however difficult that might prove.

"Um. I think she's going with a group of friends or something."

His tone and vagueness about the details lead her to believe that he never asked Lycelle. There's no way the girl would have said no.

"That's too bad. You two would have made a really cute couple."

"Will you go with me?"

Flynae swallows hard. "I wasn't necessarily going. Though Sekara might drag me. She seems to think I must suffer near her while she has fun. And wouldn't you rather attend with someone your age?" Their three-year difference might be common in the skating world, but it isn't as prevalent in high school relationships.

"Nah," Will replies, trying to be casual. "They're all full of themselves anyway. At least you know how to dance. I don't want to end up doing the slow dance shuffle all night with a ditz."

"Well, when you put it that way." Flynae laughs.

He jumps halfway in front of her, stopping her; his eyes lit up, a smile on his face. He takes both her hands in his. "Really? You'll go with me?"

"I was just going to say that I would think about it."

His beam fades. She can't handle the smell and feel of his disappointment.

"Okay. I'll go. Sekara has been talking about it for weeks now, too."

He scoops her up in a hug and spins them around. "You're the best, Fly."

She inwardly grounds. She doesn't enjoy him being so familiar. Only her brother calls her that. It's best to keep your distance from humans. "I don't like it when you call me that."

He sets her down and playfully elbows her. "Yes, you do."

As she wanders the hallway towards her next class, she wonders how she'll keep this hidden from Eksar. Even though he isn't around much lately, just a few distracted days a week, he seems to ruin anything special in her life. He'd raped her the night after she and Will had won their last competition.

She feels his hand wrap around her ankle and shudders.

28

Limo (Flynae)

On the day of the dance, Flynae and Sekara rush home to get ready. Because Eksar isn't there, they dress in Sekara's room and take turns doing each other's hair.

Since Flynae had been diligently practicing her energy manipulation skills and was now able to maintain a human appearance with just mild effort, she decides to wear her hair pulled back from her face. Her sister braids her hair for her in intricate, traditional Kaliah style.

Sekara was and is more interested in attracting the attention of boys at school than practicing energy work. Flynae arranges her sister's hair in a way to hide her ears and frames her face with long ringlets. Both girls finish their 'dos with little white flowers around the crown of their heads.

Flynae's dress has a velvet green corset bodice with a square neckline and a satin ribbon that ties behind her neck. The iridescent black skirt is floor-length and flows with her as she moves. The whole dress is brightened by intricate golden thread work throughout it. Sekara laces up the black satin ribbons that tie the corset top on Flynae.

Sekara's dress is a matching style, but the bodice is a warm gold that matches her eyes. Tonight, she wears contacts that hide the shape of her eyes as she does at school when Eksar is gone for several days in a row. They still allow the natural color to show through.

When they're both dressed and finished primping, the twins stand together before a mirror that fills the back of Sekara's bedroom door.

"Crush me," Sekara swears after taking in the sight of both of them. "We look hot."

Flynae's stomach flops within her. She grins nervously in response to her sister. They're going to attract way more attention than she wants at the dance. Will is not going to be able to take his eyes off her. He already stares at her more than she would like.

Her smile fades. She shouldn't have let Sekara talk her into such a fancy dress.

"No, no, no," Sekara says sternly while shaking her head, causing Flynae to start.

Flynae meets her sister's gaze in the mirror.

"Only happy faces tonight," Sekara responds while holding up a single scolding finger.

If only to please Sekara, Flynae assumes a convincing fake smile.

Sekara glances at the clock. "They should be here any time." She squeals and spins allowing her skirt to billow out.

The doorbell rings.

"Here we go." Sekara grabs Flynae's hand and pulls her down the stairs.

Will and Sekara's date Aster stand together on the front porch. Both boys' jaws drop when they see the girls.

"This is going to be fun," Sekara whispers to her sister. She seems to enjoy teasing humans with how beautiful she is, but Flynae doesn't see the fun. She wouldn't appreciate an elf similarly toying with her.

Will offers his arm, and Flynae accepts. The four of them climb into the limo the boys rented for the evening.

"You look lovely," Will whispers to her when he can find his voice.

His attempts at being proper and formal make her smile. "Thank you." A hint of heat touches her cheek as she inhales and smells how enamored he is with her. Still, her overwhelming emotion is one of sadness. She hates stories of unrequited love.

Aster pops a bottle of champagne, pours it into four flutes, and hands them out.

"Where did you get alcohol?" Sekara asks her date with sultry, half-lidded eyes, holding the glass close to her lips.

"My parents have so much they won't notice a bottle missing here or there."

"Do you drink?" Will asks Flynae quietly as he holds his drink and looks at it suspiciously.

"I've had wine before. My uncle makes it. You don't have to drink it if you don't want to." Kaliah have different customs concerning alcohol than most humans do as it doesn't affect them the same.

"More for me," Sekara laughs as she feigns an attempt to snatch Will's glass from him.

"If you want more alcohol," Aster tells them, though he is mostly talking to Sekara, "Eric is having a party at his house next weekend. We could all go together. I hear it's a costume party."

"We should go," Sekara shouts, bouncing up and down in her seat like an excited small child.

"We weren't invited," Flynae says, hoping, however slim the chance, that this is a sufficient out.

"I just invited you," Aster replies. "Anyone can come. I mean, at least the cool kids can come. No losers, of course. It is Erik's house after all."

Sekara grabs her sister's hand. "It will be so fun to go costume shopping together."

Flynae is a little uneasy about the idea of going to Erik's house. She did recently reject going to the dance with him. He didn't respond well to that.

"Say you'll come, Flynae." Sekara gives her sister her best puppy dog eyes.

Flynae turns to Will. "Are you going?"

He shrugs, trying to play it cool, but he focuses on her intently. "I will if you are."

Flynae sighs and tells herself it won't be that terrible if Will is there as a buffer. When they're together, he never leaves her side, making it easier for her to attend human functions. "Okay, fine."

"Hurray!" Sekara lifts her flute into the air, and they all clink glasses with her.

29

The Dance (Flynae)

The school gym is decorated to look like a place straight out of a fairytale. Soft string lights drape across the ceiling and down the walls entwined and muted by cream tulle.

Music greets them as they enter, and Flynae is delighted to see that Will's brother Ryen and his band have been hired to play for the dance.

She turns to Will. "Why didn't you tell me? When did they get the gig?"

Will blinks, seeming to come out of a slight trance. His eyes are focused intensely on her. "Uhh. They just found out yesterday. The lead of the first band got sick or something."

Flynae's body tightens under Will's stare. Why does he have to look at her that way? He smells like a cross between love and infatuation. Her heart hurts for him knowing that he'll never be anything but a really good friend to her. Romantic love with a human is out of the question for her.

Sekara waves and blows Flynae a kiss as she pulls Aster out onto the dance floor. Flynae isn't ready to be that close with

Will yet.

"Want to get some punch?" It's a lame excuse but the best she can think of at the moment.

"Whatever you want."

She clenches her hand into a fist, takes a deep breath, and lets it out. This is a bad idea. The setting is too romantic. Will is falling hard tonight, and she doesn't like it.

They stand with their cups near the wall and watch. Sekara might not be trained as a dancer, but she has the natural beauty and grace of a Kaliah which draws the room's attention.

Flynae enjoys watching her sister dance but quickly realizes she would be a lot more comfortable if she were out there as well. Dancing takes her mind off the rest of the world. She can get lost in the music, and everything else fades out. She drains her glass.

"You ready?"

Will hasn't taken his eyes off her. "For?"

"To dance with me, silly." Dancing typically helps him focus a bit more on his own body; she hopes it will do that now. She grabs his hand and leads him out. The circle created around Sekara and her partner expands to include them as well. More couples stop and stand and watch.

One of her ivory white hands is enveloped in his ebony hand. The rest of the room fades away. The music moves her as she keeps her eyes on Will's face.

After a few minutes, the lights dim and a slow song begins. Will pulls her in for a sway.

She steps back, reclaiming her space. "Huh-uh. That isn't really dancing, Will."

"You're right."

She sees the disappointment in his eyes but remains resolute.

She's rescued by a hand on her arm and turns to see Ryen's girlfriend, Carmi.

"Hey, Ryen wants you to come sing a couple of duets with him."

Flynae raises her brows. "What?" She turns and looks at the stage. When Ryen sees her eyes land on him, he nods his head emphatically.

About once a week, she and Will would take a break from skating practice and hang out at his house and listen to Ryen and his band. It was common for someone to ask her to play for them and for Ryen to ask her to sing with him. She'd never expected to be included in any public performances.

"I don't know." Somehow singing in front of a room full of people feels much different than dancing in front of them. Watching a Kaliah move is intoxicating but hearing one sing could be spellbinding. She'd always kept herself a bit restrained when singing in front of them, but she'd need to lose herself in the song to forget that all eyes were on her.

Carmi pulls her arm, and Ryen begins waving her up. Flynae relents and walks up onto the stage. Every head in the room turns in her direction. Those on the dance floor pause, watching, waiting. She smells their desire. They know something remarkable is about to happen, like they've been waiting their whole lives to hear her sing.

She takes the microphone that Kris hands her and senses the crowd holding their breath. When the first note passes her lips, they collectively relax and exhale.

She sings two duets with Ryen and then tries to bow out of more. He and his band rile up the crowd who demand an encore. The band plays a solo for her.

The applause, as she flees the stage, holding her skirt so she doesn't trip over it in her hurry, is deafening to her ears. Girls and boys alike whistle, cheer, and hoot. Her cheeks burn. The smell of the room makes her stomach ill. The overwhelming scent is lust with an underlying spoiled musty smell of jealousy. All the guys, and some of the girls, want to *do* her. The rest of the girls are resentful that they can't be her.

Sekara waits for her at the bottom of the steps and grabs her hand. "You have to come with me."

"What's up?"

She laughs. "It's Will."

Flynae's immediately concerned. "Is he all right?"

"You'll see."

The couples in the room begin to dance as the band starts playing again.

Will stands in the middle of the dance floor, staring up at the spot on the stage that she had just left. He doesn't turn or notice the girls as they approach him.

"What's wrong with him?"

At the sound of Flynae's voice, Will's eyes turn to her, but he has an empty, charmed gaze.

"I think he's under your spell." Sekara laughs again.

30

Black Eye (Flynae)

Flynae squeezes her eyes shut in exasperation. "How do I fix him?" She'd read before that, like elves, Kaliah can unwittingly cast a trance-like state over humans. It's especially common when the human has an intense desire for the immortal, but it can happen to any human who observes them when they're dancing or singing.

Flynae is familiar with the story of Amasa, a three-thousand-year-old elf who charmed an entire village of humans including those who were indoors and couldn't even see him; however, those things aren't supposed to happen until an immortal is much older.

She reaches out and takes Will's hands. His eyes blink once. Then twice. Finally, they flutter in quick succession to lubricate his eyes.

"What happened?" He looks around to get his bearings. "I feel like I just blacked out."

"I think you did." Flynae can't hold back an embarrassed smile, try as she might. Her cheeks flush.

Will shakes his head. "It wasn't a blackout." His eyes meet

hers intensely. "You were there."

Sekara giggles.

Flynae glares at her before turning back to Will. "Do you want to go get some air?" It's abruptly too warm in the room.

"Yes, please."

She takes his hand and leads him through the crowd and out a side door that had been covered by tulle. As they walk, she sighs and ponders how to stop that from ever happening again.

The door has barely closed shut behind Will when she hears a hollow thunk and Will yelp.

She turns around to see Will holding a hand to his eye and Eric next to him gloating.

Eric looks at her, his eyes narrowed and angry. "This is the loser you turned me down for?" He points at Will while taking a step toward her.

Flynae's heart quickens and her body trembles with rage. How dare he hit Will. She's seeing every detail around her tinged in red. The crimson seeps through her human disguise; and Eric stops, his eyes widening in fear.

With very little forethought to her actions, Flynae steps right up to him, their faces a few inches apart because she is six inches shorter than him. He looks expectant, his lips slightly parted, as if they are lovers about to kiss.

She draws her arm back and plows her fist forward into his gut. All his air whooshes out of him, and he doubles over. He would fall over, except she grabs his shoulders, holding him there as she brings her knee up into his groin. His mouth opens, but no sound escapes his lips. She gives him a shove, and he falls over backward to the ground.

"Leave my friends alone," she shouts at him. Her chest rises and falls rapidly as she focuses on breathing to allow her anger to dissipate.

"You're...going...to pay...for this,...bitch," Eric manages between ragged, gasping breaths.

With one hand, she gathers her skirts, with the other, she takes Will's hand again. The two of them run through the field and into the trees at the edge of the schoolyard. Will holds his other hand over his eye the whole time.

"You were amazing," he says to her when they stop.

She shrugs and places her hand on his arm to pull it from his face. "Let me see you."

He lowers his hand to reveal an angry, swollen black eye.

She inhales sharply feeling how much it hurts. "Lean down a little."

Will frowns with his good eye but bends forward until she can comfortably reach his face. She places one hand flat over the front of the injured eye and the other on the back of his head.

"What are you-"

"Shh." She closes her eyes and begins to pull the angry, inflammatory energy from his swollen face. It flows down her arms. For a moment, she experiences agony, reminiscent of the initial trauma, before it disperses from her. When she feels no more pain, she removes her hands from his head and examines her work. He looks as he was before he was hit without any trace of injury.

"What did you do?" His eyes widen in awe of her. He reaches up and gingerly, at first, touches his eye which shows no signs of Eric hitting it.

Flynae grins, feeling giddy. It's the most extensive wound she has ever healed before.

He's still bent over, his face inches from hers. Without

warning, he leans in, one arm going around her waist pulling her to him, his other to her cheek, and kisses her.

She jerks backward, pulling from his embrace, and slaps him. Even though she knew he was eventually going to kiss her, it still feels like a betrayal.

"Crush you, Will." She turns and runs through the trees, away from him and the school.

"Flynae, come back," he calls after her. "I'm sorry."

31

Panther and Fox (Flynae)

Ugh, why am I doing this? Flynae follows Sekara through a busy mall knowing they're headed to the oddball store that has everything from gag gifts, adult games, bachelor and bachelorette party supplies, sexy costumes, goth makeup, punk jewelry, and more.

She hasn't told her sister what happened between Will and her the night of the dance. When Sekara asked, with a few quick eyebrow raises suggesting something interesting had happened, where they had disappeared to that night, Flynae replied that she didn't know where Will had gone, but that she had gone to get some air and ultimately decided to walk home.

Sekara is skipping with excitement by the time they reach the store. "By the gods, look at these," she squeals, seeing their window display of slinky animal costumes.

Five mannequins dressed up in different prints and colors of furry, knee-high boots, sleek corsets with short furry skirts, furry hoods, and furry wrist warmers stand at the front of the store.

Flynae silently groans as Sekara drags her inside, knowing

that she's going to be forced to at least try on one of the skimpy outfits.

"We have to get these." Sekara's words leave no room for arguing. "It'll be like we're matching, but not." She holds up a black fuzzy costume that must be representing a panther or black cat of some sort. "Isn't it amazing? It matches my hair."

"Are you really going to wear that?" Flynae's stomach balls up within her at the thought of wearing something so revealing. She might have different thoughts about it if Eksar didn't take monthly liberties with her body.

"Why wouldn't I?" She turns to her sister with raised chin and eyebrows in a comically questioning look.

Flynae smiles and looks back at what Sekara is holding. "It's lacking–cloth." They share a laugh.

"Don't be a prude. Try one on with me."

Flynae pulls out another black one with a white stripe down the back of the hood and to the end of the thick tail. "This is cute."

"No." Sekara snatches it from her and throws it back on the rack before rifling through the rest of them. "My sister will not go as a skunk." She holds up a rusty, red costume. "Here you go. It's a little light for your hair, but I think you can make it work."

Flynae reluctantly takes it. "I'm a fox?"

"A foxy fox, for sure. Let's go try them on." She dashes off towards the dressing rooms.

Flynae follows a bit more slowly.

"Come on, Flynae. Step lively."

Flynae stands in front of the mirror trying to pull the tiny skirt down as far as it will go. "This barely covers my ass." She stares at her long lean dancer's legs in the mirror and knows, with a heavy, sinking feeling, just what Will and Eric will think of the outfit. Her throat tightens. This isn't a good idea, especially after what happened at the dance.

Sekara moves close to her twin and runs her hands over her butt. "Yeah. Isn't it great? Every guy there will want a piece of this."

Flynae stares at her sister in the mirror. "Really? You're only fourteen. Don't be such a slut."

"It's better than being a frigid bitch." Sekara giggles.

"What are you talking about?"

"It's what Eric's calling you."

Flynae rolls her eyes. That boy is a thorn in her life that won't go away.

"Do you know what happened to him?" Sekara flips her hair back and holds it in several different styles as she studies herself in the mirror.

"What do you mean?" Flynae struggles to keep a straight face not wanting Sekara to suspect anything.

Sekara turns to her sister dropping her hair and placing her hands on her hips. "How could you miss the funny way he was walking at school this week?"

"I try not to pay attention to him." Eric was another reason that Flynae thought it was a bad idea for her to go to this party. He was going to want revenge for what she did to him the night of the dance.

"Frigid bitch, huh?" Flynae turns back to look at herself in the mirror. Not because of wanting to see more of the revealing costume her sister is going to make her wear, but because she doesn't want her sister to know she had anything to do with it. "Maybe I should go get that polar bear one then. That would be more suitable for a frigid bitch."

"No way," Sekara exclaims with a pout. "The fox one is adorable. I'm getting this one. Let's change and go."

***

Flynae wakes up with her stomach in knots the morning of the dreaded costume party. Something worse than what happened at the dance is going to happen; nervous tension strains every muscle in her.

The next thing she notices is that Lord Thyde is on the planet. Her body buzzes from his nearby energy, but it's calming.

She wants to pass by the capitol building before or after school just to feel his presence even stronger. She tells herself that would be silly. And how would she explain it if he were to notice? She sighs and vows to resist even as his energy pulls and calls to hers.

After school, she puts on the horribly short, rusty red-colored skirt, and the tension in her middle builds.

What has got you all in knots today? His voice is calm and soothing in the midst of her storm. She badly wanted to talk to him but felt like her teenage angst was something fleeting that didn't need to be immortalized in conversation.

It's just a party.

He puts more of his attention on her when she responds. *And you're wearing that?* He sounds surprised but has kept any disapproval from his tone.

She lowers her eyes so he can't see her in the mirror. *Sekara wants me to.*

He deftly moves on knowing he has contributed to her discomfort. *And why does this party cause you so much disquiet?*

She tilts her head and thinks. *It's just a feeling I have. A feeling like–* She hears his boots thudding on the paved streets; her heart matches the energy, pounding in her chest. It's a similar feeling to the one she had that morning when she saw her father fall in front of her. This one isn't nearly as intense.

She opens her eyes, not even remembering that she had closed them. She's on her knees on the floor, tears streaming down her cheeks.

He doesn't apologize. He's done it so many times that she has asked him not to do it anymore. *Would it help if I stayed in town tonight?*

What? She blinks rapidly, clearing her eyes.

I'm done here at 1800, but I'll stay close instead of returning to my ship.

You would do that? A comforting warmth spread through her washing away some of the distress concerning the evening and heartache from the memory.

Always.

32

Party (Flynae)

Flynae and Sekara walk into the house together, but the dark-haired sister quickly finds a cluster of boys to surround herself with. Flynae wanders through the rooms, away from the dance floor where the music is obnoxiously loud for her keen ears until she finds Will. He's the only one besides Sekara that she would want to hang out with.

The two of them had made up Monday at school. Will had apologized for kissing her. Flynae had apologized for slapping him. And for running off and leaving him.

They had hugged and made up but skating practice was still awkward for her during the week. She found herself watching him more closely, knowing that it was going to happen again at some point.

His smell when he's around her had permanently changed after the kiss. Or was it after the trance? It was difficult to tell. As much as she hated to admit it, she presumed that he was full-blown in love with her.

Smelling him now causes her physical pain. Her throat closes up. Her eyes threaten tears. Her stomach clenches. She never wanted to hurt him. Now she finds herself backed into an impossible corner, and the only way out is to break his heart. Thinking about it makes her want to puke.

"Woah." Will's eyes widen when he sees her and takes his time admiring the costume and all her perfect skin that it displays. "That's quite the getup."

Flynae stiffens and resists tugging on the horribly short skirt. She told herself if she was going to wear the outfit then she wasn't going to fidget with it all night. Besides, she was wearing a pair of dance shorts underneath. It wasn't like more of her was going to be revealed if she had a clothing malfunction. "Sekara made me wear it."

"Mmm. Tell Sekara I approve."

She shoves his chest hard enough that he has to take a step back to avoid falling over and grins at her. She exhales and can't stop herself from smiling back; the boy has a great smile. It makes her happy.

They move to a corner out of the middle of the room. People still stare at them. Boys and girls alike run their eyes over her smooth, flawless legs. They look at Will with jealousy.

Flynae stands closer to him than she would like, close enough to feel the warmth of his body. He's a safer place for her than the rest of the room. The smell of desire coming off him intensifies when she turns and their elbows touch. The emotion is frantic. It says that he will do anything for her if he only knew what she wanted him to do. She wants him to fall in love with a human girl. The only way for that to happen is for them to spend less to no time together. She's going to need to let him go soon.

Sekara saves Flynae from the agony in her mind when she

shows up with two red plastic cups in her hand. "Here, guys. Have a drink." She shoves the beverages toward them.

"What is it?" Flynae takes the drink to avoid it spilling on her and inhales. The top aroma is fruity while underneath is the unpleasant smell of strong booze.

"Alcohol, of course." Sekara rolls her eyes at them feigning annoyance. "What is a party without it?"

"A coordinated one." Flynae smirks.

Will chuckles at her joke.

Flynae looks at Will. He raises his glass in salute and takes a sip first and then a gulp. "Woah, that's strong." He grimaces.

Flynae stifles the laugh in her throat. It's not his fault humans can't handle their drink. She takes a sip and pronounces it not too terrible.

"That's it." Sekara nods her approval. "Don't waste it." She flits off as quickly as she arrived.

Flynae wonders what they're doing there. Will only came because she did. She only came because Sekara wanted it. She doesn't have any desire to talk with anyone here.

The teenagers stand around the room in small groups clutching their plastic cups in their hands. The girls try to be coy and flirtatious, twirling their hair around their fingers or pushing up their boobs when they think no one is looking. Some of the guys pretend to be only mildly interested to come across as suave. The room is thick with the scent of people wanting to get into each other's pants.

The music blares so loudly that she has to shout for Will to hear her if she talks. She can tune the music out and hear any conversation happening in the house if she desired to.

In the middle of her people watching, she notices a familiar scent coming from near her. She turns and sees Will leaning back to look at her legs.

"Gods!" She playfully elbows him. "Can you please keep your hormones to yourself?"

"Sorry." He brings his eyes up to meet hers. "You did check the mirror before you left, right?"

"Yes. I'm painfully aware that my body has about as much cloth on it as the average streetwalker." Once again, she regrets her outfit decision and decides to make the best of it. "I'm bored. Want to go dance? Shake my tail a bit." She shimmies her hips, and her fox tail sways.

"Heck yes." He would never deny her a dance. They hold hands to traverse the room of bodies and enter the one where the music is pounding. Sweaty teenagers are doing something that they consider dancing. She sees it as drunk people swaying about.

Flynae and Will each take a large gulp and set their drinks on a table off to the side of the room. A space clears as the two begin to move. They perform for each other, pulling out all their hip-hop moves, forgetting everything around them.

They're both glistening and out of breath when Will yawns and shakes his head.

Flynae puts her lips up to his ear. "Are you okay?"

"I think I'm just tired. Can we go sit down?"

"Can't handle your liquor?" She laughs.

"It was just one drink. I guess it was stronger than I thought."

Flynae gives the couple making out on the couch a little energetic push as she and Will enter the room, and they vacate the space.

He flops down. "I just need to sit for a bit." He leans back and closes his eyes.

She sits on the arm of the couch next to him. "I think exercise makes your body process it faster." She takes his hand and checks his pulse. It's coming down from the exertion, but nothing about it worries her.

"What's wrong with him?" Sekara stands next to her again and shoves a drink into her hand.

"I think it was too strong for him. I don't think he drinks a lot."

"I'm a dancer; I must respect my body," Sekara says mockingly, earning her a glare from her sister. "It's fine. More for us." She clinks glasses with her twin, takes a sip with her, and then darts away again.

Flynae sits and nurses her cocktail while keeping an eye on Will. Sleeping it off is probably the best thing for him. His breathing and pulse are steady so she isn't too concerned.

The feeling of someone's eyes crawling over her skin causes her eyes to fly open. She realizes she doesn't remember closing them in the first place, and the trepidation of something awful happening comes back like a punch in the gut, taking her breath away.

Her drink is still in her lap. Will is leaning with his head against her hip snoring softly. The room spins around her. Nothing feels normal. She could have been drinking straight alcohol and never responded to it like this.

She scans her surroundings. Across the room, halfway up the stairs, Eric sits watching her through the balusters, a smirk on his face.

Flynae sets her glass aside and struggles to her feet. Her body has never felt this heavy before, even after hitting her head. She staggers to the kitchen where she finds Sekara laughing in the middle of a circle of boys. Flynae pushes one of them aside and grabs her sister's upper arm.

"Who gave you my drinks?" She has to concentrate to not slur her words.

"Are you okay?" Sekara furrows her brows in worry.

"Who gave you my drinks? To give to me?"

"Eric. Why?"

Flynae doesn't even have to turn around to know that Eric has followed her, keeping her in his sight. She shakes her head and glares at Sekara before heading to the front door.

"What?" Sekara calls after her, shrugs when there is no response, and then turns her attention back to the boys near her.

The house spins around her, and Flynae barely keeps herself upright. She wonders if she's walking on the floor or the walls. Fresh air hits her face when she pulls the front door open and walks out. She inhales deeply, hoping to clear her head a little.

"Where do you think you're going?" Eric calls from behind her.

She doesn't turn around. The motion would make her head spin worse. She senses three other boys standing with him.

She quickens her pace and attempts to run. They'll never be able to catch her if she can run. From the sound of their steps behind her, they're catching her. In her distracted drugged state, her boot toe catches on the sidewalk, and she stumbles sideways into the grass.

Eric stands over her when she looks up. He holds up his hands for the other guys to wait. "I've got this."

She rolls over and manages to get to her feet. The two of them scuffle. Everything is a blur; she barely knows what is happening. Something makes a horrible snapping sound and Eric begins screaming. His friends come rushing in and shove her to the ground.

She barely notices them as the sound of authoritative footsteps approaching takes precedence over everything else. Her heart races; terror clutches her lungs in an icy grip.

33

My Lady (Kovad)

Lord Thyde had his pilot park the shuttle at the air pad in the neighborhood where the party was taking place. From there, he could continue to work while being roughly a mile away.

He found himself distracted from his reports by concern when Sekara brought Flynae the first drink but chose to swallow his disapproval. She didn't need him telling her what to do. His chosen role in her life was to keep her safe if he could no matter what she did.

As she headed to the dance floor with Will, Lord Thyde turned his attention back to the construction reports from sector 6. The battleship plant was behind on production, and the general in charge was making excuses. This meant he was either hiding something or was incompetent. No matter what, a demotion was coming his way quickly. In the meantime, Lord Thyde dove into the details to see exactly where things were going wrong.

He's abruptly pulled out of his concentration when Flynae opens her eyes and realizes she'd been falling asleep. He feels the tension in her core as keenly as if it were happening in his body.

He waves his hand, and the reports on the hologram disappear. In a few quick strides, he's outside. "With me," he says to the two guards. They fall in behind him, matching his pace, as he begins swiftly jogging.

When he hears Sekara admit that Eric supplied the drinks for Flynae, he starts running. His heart beats faster than the exertion calls for as he sees through her eyes that she is followed from the house. He quickens his pace again, and his guards begin struggling to keep up. They don't have the benefit of channeling the energy flowing around them to their use.

His fists clench when Flynae falls, and Eric stands over her. That boy might not even glance in her direction ever again when he is through with him tonight.

Lord Thyde sees her now, struggling with Eric, still several houses away. The boy shrieks in pain, and a thrill of approval flows through Kovad. The other boys pull her away, throw her to the ground, and hold her there.

The pounding of his footsteps becomes the only thing he hears as it becomes the sole focus of her attention. Even though he is keeping an entirely different pace and gait from that day when he killed her father, it's like his steps have a consistent signature that her ears detect. He feels her terror and pain at the sound of his arrival gripping his spine. He hates it; hates that his approach causes her such anguish; hates that there is nothing he can do to change it; hates the helplessness he's left with. He channels the helplessness to ire at the people hurting her now.

Eric and his accomplices look up with stunned expressions as Lord Thyde comes to a stop just fifteen feet from them. His guards catch up seconds later and flank him.

"Stun those three boys." He points at the ones holding Flynae.

Each guard fires two shots from their gun. The boy in the middle is hit twice.

Kovad's anger boils within him as he walks with calm, commanding steps right up to Eric. Flynae rolls onto her side and puts her hands over her ears, responding to the sound of his stride. *She'll be all right in a moment,* he tells himself.

Lord Thyde grabs Eric by the neck and lifts him straight up off the ground. Eric lets go of the arm he'd been cradling to grab Kovad's wrist with his good arm. His other arm dangles and is broken in at least one place.

"If I hear of you or anyone else at your school coming near her again without her permission, I will personally castrate you in front of the entire school. Do I make myself clear?"

"Ya-a-a," Eric croaks.

Lord Thyde abruptly releases him to fall to the ground and shriek again from landing on his arm, knowing that he wasn't going to be able to stop himself from visibly trembling with rage much longer. He pulls his cloak off his shoulders and places it over Flynae before pulling her into his arms.

She fights against him, but he knows it's just instinct from being chased by the boys.

He leans down and whispers to her, "It's me. I'm here. I've got you, Flynae."

She inhales, smells him, and relaxes.

He stands, holding her as tightly to him as he dares without risking hurting her, and turns to his guards. "There is a black teenage boy passed out on a couch just inside. Secure him and wait with him until an ambulance arrives."

With a nod, they move to obey.

He carries her back to his shuttle and holds her while he calls ahead to the Imperialist Hotel.

"I need your most expensive available room for the evening." There was no need for him to give his name. Their communication system would show the call was coming from his shuttle.

"The penthouse suite is available."

"Perfect. I also need some clothes for a size 2 female. 5'2". Elegant bohemian style. Bring three options. Leggings and a tunic, floor-length skirt, and whatever else your stylist thinks fits the description."

"The penthouse is ready for your arrival. I have someone working on the clothes now. Is there anything else we can provide for you, my lord?" The clerk had recognized the voice he was hearing by now.

Kovad looks down at her sleeping face. He'd like to order her some food, but she probably won't wake up until morning. He can't resist stroking her hair. It falls back at his touch, and he sees a bruise beginning to show on her jawline. His fury rises again. Those boys are lucky they got away as they did. He's in the mood now to flog them publicly. His hand clenches around an imagined whip handle.

Flynae whimpers and tenses.

Just rest. You're safe. He forces himself to relax.

"Not unless you can acquire kya leaf," he tells the hotel clerk.

"Actually, yes. We have other high-profile guests who request that as well. There is a shop down the street that carries it. I'll send someone. How much would you like?"

Kovad finds this curious. What Kaliah are high-profile guests at the hotel? He realizes he doesn't know what amount of kya should be ordered at a time. "An average amount is fine."

"Consider it done." The clerk deftly skips over his vague answer. "What else might we do for you, my lord?"

"That will be all."

"It has been my pleasure, my lord."

The guards return to the shuttle shortly after the comm to the hotel ends, and the pilot navigates them to the rooftop landing pad.

As he holds her in the elevator while it descends one floor from the roof, he can't help but feel a little sadness at letting her go.

The attendant opens the door to the suit for him. He takes her to the massive bed, moves the chocolates from the turndown service to the nightstand, and sets her down. He leaves his cloak around her, pulls off her furry boots, and tucks her in.

"Sleep well, my lady."

Her pulse quickens in her sleep at the sound of his steps walking away.

34

Cloak (Flynae)

The sun is shining and the room is brightly lit with natural light when Flynae awakes. It is a welcome contrast to the cold, dark basement she has become accustomed to.

The second thing she notices is an intoxicating fragrance. She inhales again, focusing on it while ignoring the stronger scent of the clean linens. She pushes back the plush duvet and sees that she is wrapped in a black cloak. His cloak. The exhilarating scent is coming from it.

She brings the fabric to her nose and inhales again. The predominant smell is his rich, strong, musky, everyday fragrance. What caught her attention the most was a sweeter smell, the faint top-note that he had imparted to the garment last night. That aroma meant affection and attraction with a dash of possessiveness.

Her throat tightens as she holds back her own emotions. These are the smells that she longs to have in her life every day. She wants someone to feel those ways about her.

To distract herself from a potential pity party, she sits,

throws back the covers, and takes in more of her surroundings. The sparsely furnished bedroom is ornately detailed and massive. Flynae wonders why anyone would need such a large room to sleep in.

Keeping the cloak around her, she scoots to the edge of the bed. Upon seeing the fury boots on the floor near the wall, her cheeks burn. She's still wearing that ridiculous fox costume from last night.

Flashes of the previous evening start coming back to her. She remembers Sekara bringing her a drink and dancing with Will for a while. Eric chased her through the house and outside. Her heartbeat quickens at the memory. Who knows what he would have done if he'd caught her. His eyes conveyed such malice. But he had caught her, she wonders. Those details are fuzzy.

Lord Thyde had been there. He'd carried her away from them. Her hands tremble as she grips the fabric of his robe, closes her eyes, and inhales his scent again to calm her. He'd kept her safe when she was unable to do so for herself. She wishes she had been awake to appreciate his presence.

When she looks back at her surroundings, she notices the nearby clothing.

Was there something you didn't think of? she wonders as she holds up the leggings and tunic and sees that they will fit perfectly.

She makes her way into the sizable bathroom. The tub looks big enough to comfortably hold four people.

She sheds her clothing and steps into the spacious black and white marble-tiled shower. The hot water warms and refreshes her. She turns it almost as hot as it will get, and the room quickly fills with steam.

She only allows herself a few minutes under the scalding water. Who knows if she is missed at home and, if she is, what sort of punishment she's in for.

After she's dry and dressed, she wraps his cloak around her again, unwilling to be apart from it, and ventures out into the living area of the massive suite.

An elegant food cart sits there waiting for her. Under the silver lids atop it, she finds fresh fruits, raw fish, raw eggs, fresh-squeezed juices, and delicate breakfast pastries. It's enough food for several.

She blinks rapidly thinking about how much money he spent for her to have a safe place to sleep for the night. The action was extravagant, overwhelming, and endearing.

She places a little of everything onto a plate and walks out onto the balcony to eat.

The view of the city from up there on the fiftieth floor is breathtaking. The city sprawls out in front of her. Her keen eyes can see all the way down to the Underground beneath the cement facade. The noise of the city is like din in the background. For once, she almost feels at peace in the large, busy city of Solum.

When her breakfast is finished, she sighs and forces herself to get up. The longer she avoids returning to where she lives, the angrier Eksar will be–if he is home at all. She's praying that he isn't.

As she looks around at all the fine furniture and bright open space of the suite, she reflects that it was nice to pretend for a short while that she belonged there.

When she reaches the door to walk out, she realizes that she still has Lord Thyde's cloak around her shoulders. She can't take it home. Eksar can't know about their association. There is no telling what he would do.

Flynae acknowledges that she has no choice but to leave the robe behind. She gathers it together in her arms and buries her face in it. As she inhales, her knees weaken, and she lowers herself to the floor. There are very few things she has ever wanted to hold onto as badly as she wants to keep this length of black fabric.

Silent tears flow down her cheeks.

After a few minutes, she dries her eyes with her sleeve, folds the cloak and places it on the back of the couch, holds her head high, and walks from the room.

35

Bite (Flynae)

Eksar was not home when Flynae arrived. Her sister, however, had been very distraught while waiting for her. Sekara threw herself into Flynae's arms, almost knocking her over when she walked through the front door.

"I was so worried about you," the dark-haired girl exclaims. "I had no idea Eric was going to drug you. Are you okay?" She steps back, holding Flynae by the shoulders, and takes a good look at her sister. "Where have you been? And where did you get those cute clothes?"

"I was provided with a place to stay and a change of clothes from a...friend." It was strange to say the word aloud when talking about him, but she realized how true it was.

"A friend?" Sekara's eyes narrow. "Will is the only person I ever see you hanging out with. And after you ran outside, he had Imperial guards standing watch over him until an emergency vehicle arrived."

"Is he okay?" *Is Will okay?* Flynae was ashamed that she had been too distracted that morning to ask about him before now.

"How should I know?" Sekara throws up her hands. "I

haven't seen him since he was taken away on a stretcher."

The boy is fine. He was in stable condition and released this morning.

Flynae releases all the air from her lungs. Her shoulders relax, but her stomach tightens with a fury of butterflies within her. His attention to the details that concerned her the previous evening was overwhelming. He must have checked on Will before she even asked because he had an answer at the ready.

"Are you okay?"

Flynae realizes she's staring at nothing while she's trying to get a handle on her emotions and looks up to see Sekara frowning. "I'm fine. Last night was just a little...scary. Terrifying." Suddenly angry, she puts an index finger before her sister's face. "Don't you ever give me something from someone else like that again." Her anger burns in her eyes.

Sekara dramatically throws her hands before her face and cowers. "Okay. I'm sorry. He said he just wanted to make sure you had a good time."

Flynae shakes her head. "You're so naive."

"And you're so mistrusting of everyone."

With good reason, Flynae thinks to herself.

***

Monday morning at school brought with it a big surprise. Flynae couldn't remember much after she had fled the house at the party. She wasn't expecting to walk into school and see Eric in the shape he was in. He had a black eye, a bruise around the front of his throat, an arm in a sling, and a slight limp. Every time he or one of his louts saw her, they turned and trotted off in the other direction.

What did you do to him? She feels Lord Thyde smile when he recognizes what she's referring to and senses that he's more than a little pleased with the outcome.

I can take credit for the bruises around his neck and his strained ankle. A memory of holding Eric by his throat flashes across Lord Thyde's mind.

Flynae is impressed by his strength. As the quarterback of the high school football team, Eric is not a small person. *What about the rest of him?*

That was all you, my lady.

She blushes at his term of respect. *Do you know what I did to him then?*

According to the hospital report, he has multiple lacerations, a broken arm, and a bite wound.

How did he get a bite wound? She frowns.

He laughs. *The report said that the shape of the bite wound was fitting with that which a human would make, but the depth of the canine teeth marks was more befitting that of a large canine or feline.*

You mean..., oh gods...I bit him?

Yes. She'd expect someone's tone to be disapproving, but Lord Thyde sounds quite satisfied.

I've never bit anyone before.

I'm not sure anyone has deserved it before quite like he did.

36

Field Trip (Flynae)

Flynae wakes up Friday morning with a painful knot in her gut, her body dripping sweat. Her lower torso is aching for no reason other than a strong premonition. Something terrible is going to happen today, and she is most likely unable to do anything about it.

Eksar had returned last night, and so had Flynae's perpetual state of fear. He'd been mostly silent during dinner, answering Sekara's questions with curt or one-word answers until she'd given up trying to converse with him.

Flynae puts off going upstairs for as long as she can but knows that she will be in trouble if she isn't at breakfast by 7 am. The only reason she can fathom that he insists on eating together is purely to torture her.

When she slides into her seat at the table, he announces, "Flynae has a field trip today. She won't be going with you to school, Sekara."

Flynae's entire body clenches. Whatever he has in store for her won't be pleasant.

"Where is she going?" Sekara asks, trying to sound casual

while glancing at her sister with eyes that show a lot of white.

"Don't worry yourself, my daughter. She's going where she belongs."

Where do I belong? Flynae racks her brain for an answer as if it is a puzzle to solve. She scans back over every word that he's said in her presence. The only thing that comes close to possibly applying to this situation is him talking about her being raised for her purpose. Is this related? She struggles to swallow her breakfast.

Shortly after Sekara leaves for school, Flynae follows Eksar to his shuttle. Her trepidation has attracted Lord Thyde's attention. He constantly checks in on her situation which brings her a little comfort, but she has a strong feeling that this event is going to be beyond his abilities to intercede.

As she steps aboard the vehicle, she realizes this is the first time she has been on this craft. He has never taken her anywhere before. If it weren't for Senice, she would never have been off the planet Diomede.

The door closes behind them with a hiss, sealing them in together. The walls press in, creating a moment of claustrophobic panic from being alone with him in a confined space.

He turns to her with a malicious, wide grin that makes him look half mad.

She stands her ground, with her chin up. Shortly after he'd started taking advantage of her, she'd made a pact with herself that she wouldn't cower in his presence. He would enjoy it too much. She was still Issiah's daughter and would carry herself as such.

He rushes at her, causing her to back up until her knees hit a seat and plop down in it. Her heart races, and she works to control her rapid breaths as he reaches on either side of her hips to grab the lap belt and fasten it.

"Let's go for a ride, noble daughter."

Her ears tickle as she picks up on that clue. This does have something to do with her being of royal blood.

He moves to the cockpit, giving her space to collect herself. She hasn't a clue where they are heading except that it is up into space.

After little more than an hour, the motion changes. Her best guess is that they're landing aboard a larger ship. The movement feels different from landing on a planet.

When the shuttle comes to a stop, she unbuckles and stands up. Eksar is quickly out of the cockpit and motioning for her to follow him.

She'd seen pictures of a hanger bay in books and on the omegaweb and through Lord Thyde's eyes before, but that is a bit different than stepping into one. The massive bay holds hundreds of ships on platforms lining the sides in rows upon rows wide and high. The greyness of the room is striking. The walls are grey, the ships are grey, the rails are grey. The sight is oppressive and bleak.

The Imperial guards stand out against the drab background in their black and gold uniforms. Some of the men are wearing black and purple. These are the colors of the Emperor's personal security.

She follows Eksar down grey corridors. Finally, he presses his palm against a panel, and a door slides aside into the wall. The room inside is anything but plain. The floors are no longer metal but marble tile. The walls are warm oak wood. When she inhales, she smells the natural wood.

Two barefoot Kaliah women stand in the middle of the room, seeming to be waiting for them. They wear exotic purple silks in the style of the Emperor's mistresses: harem pants with slits from ankle to hip and bikini halter tops. Their beautiful, ageless faces are stoic, betraying no emotion.

Flynae hears the door closing behind her and glances around to see that Eksar has left. She doesn't know if she should feel relieved or not.

When she turns back, one of the Kaliah beckons her to follow with a nod of their head.

The antechamber leads to a large open room with a fountain in the middle and three other lavish rooms leading off it.

Everywhere she looks are more scantily clad girls. Most of them are humans aged fifteen to twenty-five. All of them are quite attractive, but no one is smiling. Not one of them looks happy in their elegant cage.

Flynae realizes that she recognizes the faces of some of them. She has seen them through Lord Thyde's eyes when he attended the Emperor's parties. As a lord, Kovad Thyde doesn't have a choice but to attend though he doesn't prefer being around the activities that happened there and never partook of them himself.

Emperor Seko would have his women dance and sing for his lords and often offered them up as nothing more than a toy if he was particularly pleased with one of his lords. Some of the women didn't survive being "played" with.

Flynae closes her eyes, blocking out the room, following the Kaliah by their energy alone, as she senses Lord Thyde checking in with her. He's been paying attention to her all morning, when he could, wanting to know where she was being taken.

Where are you? His thoughts are strained with tension that almost rivals hers.

I don't want you to know. Her throat hurts as she chokes back tears. Her cheeks burn with the shame of what she imagines is to come.

Please show me. We'll get through it together. She feels his torment at not knowing what is happening to her.

She opens her eyes as she's led into a large bathroom. When she glances at the two Kaliah women, he recognizes their faces though he'd only seen them behind a human disguise.

What the fuck! She feels his hands clench with his rage. His mind immediately goes to his favorite stress outlet: beating an expendable prisoner to death.

No! Please. For most of the past ten years, he's reserved carrying out punishments like that when she's asleep. Much to her horror, she had woken on many occasions to a man screaming in agony or dying.

He takes a few breaths and calms himself. *I won't ever purposely expose you to that again.*

One of the women begins filling the massive bathtub with hot steamy water that pours like a waterfall from the ceiling while the other removes her clothes. Her face and ears burn, but she doesn't resist. Because of the age difference, they're much more skilled in energy manipulation than she is in spite of her royal blood.

One day my heritage will work for me, she thinks to herself.

They wordlessly direct her to enter the tub where she's scrubbed with sugars and salts and doused with jasmine and vanilla oils. After the bath, her body is oiled, her hair is pulled back and up, and her finger and toenails are filed and glossed.

As the processes continue, Flynae becomes more and more worried about what she is possibly being prepared for. It seems like too much of a fuss if she is merely being added to a harem.

They dress her in a floor-length, purple satin, strapless dress. The bodice ties in the back, and they sinch her in pushing up her chest to create as much cleavage as possible. The skirt is full and swishes as she walks. Sparkling gold heels are placed on her feet, adding three inches to her height. Her neck is adorned with an emerald necklace that hangs just above her decolletage. Diamond flowers are placed in her hair. One of the final steps they make is to cast an energy spell over her to make her appear human.

When she sees herself in one of the many mirrors lining the salon room, she can't help but feel like a lamb being dressed for slaughter.

She's looking at herself in the mirror when a hand caresses her shoulder. She jerks away, startled, her heart racing, knowing that it wasn't one of the Kaliah women who'd just touched her. Somehow her ears hadn't alerted her to someone else approaching.

She finds herself staring into a pair of red eyes. The male before her looks both Kaliah and not. His irises are red; his pupils are round, not feline. His slender ears push up, taller than a Kaliah's, from his shoulder-length hair. His mouth widens in a leer above his square jaw.

Who the hell is that?

Flynae realizes that Lord Thyde has never seen this elf through his disguise.

That, my lord, is your Emperor.

37

The Emperor (Flynae)

H*e's an elf?* Lord Thyde asks.

A very dark elf... Flynae thinks to herself rather than in response. Emperor Seko has long scars visible on his face and neck. His presence is thick and heavy. She struggles for full breaths because of the weight of it.

What did he do to himself? She doesn't understand his wounds, his demeanor. Granted, no one really knows much about him. The Kaliah know that he has been Emperor off and on of the human world for centuries now. Every forty to eighty years, he disguises and promotes or usurps himself to maintain authority under a new name.

What does he want with you? Lord Thyde's thoughts are tense and distressed.

I can only surmise it has to do with my bloodline.

Your family is ancient. There must be other royals.

No. Not many that I can place. Besides Fennec and myself, my father's last child was born several millennia ago. I don't know of any others besides Siah. She acknowledges that she's an easy target because of her age. If Siah and Seko were to meet, who would win?

Seko holds out his arm for her. "Shall we?"

She has no choice but to wrap her arm around his. His ancient energy abilities could move her body around like a marionette if he wanted to. She wasn't about to give him the pleasure.

Flynae finds herself glancing at him sideways, looking at his scars with puzzlement. Kaliah skin heals quickly and shows no history of serious wounds. He's not a Kaliah either. The realization hits her harder the second time. He's an elf.

That doesn't feel one hundred percent accurate though. If he was, his presence wouldn't be so oppressive. Elves are kind, wise, perfect beings. They wouldn't be so cruel. Seko's brutish acts are well-known throughout the galaxy.

What are you? she wonders.

His presence continues to overwhelm her. Her feet feel like she's walking with cinder blocks attached to them. It's a stark difference from her normal weightlessness. Her breath comes with great effort.

This is intentional, she thinks to herself. Kaliah naturally have an effect over others that they can decide to suppress or limit. He is amplifying his.

He leads her to the hanger bay, and they board his waiting shuttle. He grabs her arm, sits down in a chair, and pulls her onto his lap.

She lets out the slightest gasps and her mouth falls slightly open. It takes her a moment to collect herself as her whole body clenches.

Her attention falls on Lord Thyde's focus on what is happening with her. He might as well be standing in the room watching, unable to physically respond. It's like she can see his face and the pained furrows on his brow.

As Emperor Seko's hand slides its way up her skirt over her bare skin to her thigh, she looks inwardly to Lord Thyde. *Please don't watch.* Her cheeks burn with shame. She stands even less of a chance against the Emperor than she does Eksar.

I won't let you go through anything alone.

Seko's other hand snakes around her back to land on her corseted breast. He leans into her neck and takes a deep inhale.

You're flying right now. She knows he's alone and preoccupied. Lord Thyde's first love was flying, and he often piloted his shuttle whenever he didn't need accompanied.

It's on autopilot.

He appears before her in her mind holding out his hand. She takes it and stands near his presence.

I have an idea, he thinks. Moments later, she hears music through his ears.

It's a perfect distraction for her. She can get lost in music. Everything else except for him and the sound fades away. Time passes without measure. She is almost at peace.

You've landed. His words bring her back to her body in time. She catches herself with her hands and knees to stop from face planting as she's pushed from the Emperor's lap.

A few drops of blood fall from her arm and land on the floor. Her eyes move from the red on the floor to her limb. Three angry raised bite marks stand out from the pale skin of her upper arm. The skin is broken in several places and weeps sanguine liquid.

A white cloth lands on the floor near her hand.

"Clean yourself up." The Emperor stands over her gloating. The smell of his dark delight is enough to make her stomach turn.

She holds the cloth over the wounds applying slight pressure to stop the bleeding, stifling her instinct to flinch. She'll do all she can not to add to his pleasure.

"Let's go." He holds out his arm again. Holding her head proudly, she tries not to tremble as she takes it.

38

Entrance (Kovad)

The building was originally a palace with extravagant and elegant marble floors and columns, ornate woodworking, and hand-sculpted statues. The tall windows are lined with delicate chiffon drapes to block the glare and still allow for the most natural light. Lead crystal chandeliers adorn the vaulted ceilings. A chamber orchestra plays off to the side of the main ballroom on a dais. The setting seems straight out of a fairytale if one can ignore the stuffy airs of those who take the beauty and grandeur of the artwork for granted.

Lord Thyde focuses on his breath as he waits, third in line to receive the Emperor, knowing that he needs to not let his aura give his feelings away. This may prove to be an impossible task as many strong emotions war within him already.

He has spent most of his life in awe of the Emperor, doing everything within his power to earn Seko's favor and climb the military ranks. After Kovad's father died, Seko became a parental figure to him, pushing him to his limits and bringing out his greatness.

Everything that he had built the Emperor up to be in his mind has been slowly dissolving since the day he'd killed Issiah. The last of it comes crashing down now as he struggles to keep images of what the Emperor might have in store for Flynae out of his mind.

He is one of two Lords out of the ten total that doesn't have a lady on his arm. Three of the Lords are married and stand with their trophy wives while the other five have very expensive escorts hanging onto them.

On paper, the ten Lords may be considered equals in rank as seconds in command of the galaxy, but the Emperor has always made their status in his favor apparent.

He feels her presence getting closer. It's like the warm heartbeat of a homing beacon increasing in intensity as she approaches. She takes in the splendor around her with appreciation and uses it for distraction.

Lord Thyde holds his breath as she pauses with the Emperor to wait for the great doors before them to be opened allowing them to enter the banquet hall. Then he sees her and exhales.

The room quiets. Every eye turns towards the pair. Emperor Seko now appears as his attractive, charming human facade. He has disguised Flynae as human and concealed the wounds on her arm.

As they seem to float together into the room, Lord Thyde recognizes that she has eclipsed the Emperor. Her presence is bright and strong like a spotlight shines on her while Seko is cloaked in shadow.

He watches her close her eyes and incline her head ever so slightly towards someone. One of the servers is Kaliah and has recognized and acknowledged her royal blood.

The pair approaches the first Lord. Kovad is overcome by a

possessive wave of jealousy when the Lord takes her hand and kisses the back of it.

I can smell you from here. Which means he can sense you as well. She holds herself steady while her heart pounds in her chest.

Lord Thyde focuses on bringing his emotions to neutral. The effect is only temporary as Seko leads Flynae a few steps closer. The Emperor meets his eyes, and Kovad senses rather sees a slight smirk.

He's amused. And intrigued. You should distract yourself. Her stomach is in her throat, threatening to choke her. Every muscle in her body is tense and strained.

Distract myself from looking at the most exquisite being I've ever laid eyes upon?

Then she is right before him, looking up at him with her emerald eyes. He wants nothing more at that moment than to gather her in his arms and be her human shield against any who would harm her.

He holds out his hand. She gives him hers and every nerve in both of them lights up at the touch. He brings her soft delicate skin to his lips and kisses her hand. A shiver runs through her.

"My lady."

She swallows and collects herself to speak. "My lord." She looks away, unable to continue meeting his gaze and hold herself together at the same time. Her legs tremble. Then she is no longer before him as she is led away to receive homage from the next lord.

Kovad admires her as she keeps her composure while being led through a sea of vipers on the arm of the devil.

39

Banquet (Flynae)

She noticed they stood in front of Lord Thyde slightly longer than the previous two lords. Her legs quiver like they'll rebel at holding her upright at any moment. At least she can keep her upper body under control. The bodice of her dress becomes too tight for her to catch her breath, and she struggles to not hyperventilate. Her pulse pounds in her ears.

With a slight tug on her arm, Emperor Seko signals that they are moving on. Everyone else is a blur as her focus is on Kovad, though her photogenic memory perfectly captures all the names and faces in the room.

She feels Lord Thyde's struggle to keep his eyes off her as she is paraded around and displayed to all in attendance.

I'm not here.

Like hell, you're not.

Midst the sea of other emotions, she can pick out the smell of his affection and controlled rage. Men and women alike lust after her. Some are jealous of the attention she receives being on the arm of the Emperor. No matter how they feel about her, no one can look away for long. Her skin crawls from all the eyes on her.

Finally, someone is holding a chair for her to sit down. She breathes a sigh of relief that her legs held out. A full glass of champagne is before her. She takes it and drains it in two gulps. It's immediately filled again.

Her trembling body calms the tiniest bit. The champagne might be the way she gets through the evening. She drinks half of it. It's shortly refilled again.

Lord Thyde's presence is tantalizingly close, but still too far away for her comfort. Lord One sits at Seko's right hand. Lord Two sits to her left. Kovad is on the other side of Lord One. She can't see him, and it's torment.

Briefly, she closes her eyes and can almost feel his arms wrapped around her. Her body relaxes in response. She opens her eyes and banishes the vision. Now is not the time to let her guard down. The night's suffering has barely begun.

She reaches out to pick up the champagne flute again and is aware of Lord Thyde watching her hand. He inwardly notices how small and delicate their shape is and longs to hold them in his. She hesitates until she can pick it up without the slightest quivering and empties it.

If only she could get another glimpse of him it might help her to settle. As if in answer, his hand reaches out to grasp his water glass and pauses for a moment before lifting it.

Her heart flutters and her cheeks burn at the gesture that was done purely for her benefit. She clenches a fist under the table and blinks to keep back the threatening tears.

The quivering in her core turns to nausea as the smell of dark mold assaults her nose. She looks in time to see the Emperor smirking at her, clearly enjoying her aura of turmoil.

Get it together, Flynae. What would your father think? This inner scolding serves its purpose. She straightens her back, lifts her chin, and consumes the recently poured champagne.

From the corner of her eye, she sees Kovad setting his water glass down.

No champagne for you, my lord?

I don't drink. Especially not at work.

You're always working. This is more of a thought to herself than a response to him. She knows he's working twice as hard tonight with her to keep track of.

The food service begins. An amuse of smoked salmon on a delicate crostini is placed before her with an ounce of white wine. The sight and smell of the food make her stomach roll. She might be viewed unfavorably if she doesn't eat though.

Before eating the bite before her, she takes a sip of the wine. The course has been expertly paired. The wine has a smooth, buttery feel that compliments the salmon. Before the dish is cleared, she finishes the wine.

The courses keep coming: a terrine of crab, a Caprese salad, a carpaccio of the most expensive beef in the galaxy, a chilled potato soup, and on and on. She has at least a bite of everything and finishes all the wine.

By the time that dessert arrives, she has consumed enough wine and champagne that all her strong emotions are dulled. She can look at Lord Thyde's hand without falling apart with desire for the safety and comfort they would provide her. And she can handle every malicious scent coming from the Emperor without a shudder or tremble.

Her throat still feels as if someone is gripping it to choke her when the banquet is over and it is time to rise and leave. Her skin crawls as she takes the Emperor's arm once more. She holds her head high as he leads her to his shuttle.

40

I'm Here (Kovad)

As soon as the doors close between Kovad and Flynae with the Emperor, he rushes to find a side exit out of the building towards his shuttle. He knows she's going to need him. And soon.

The staff looks at him with wide eyes, wondering why he is invading their work spaces, before jumping out of his way. He barely sees them; anything but the way marked by red exit signs is a blur.

His heart sets a racing pace to keep in step with hers. Her fear is palpable enough that it causes him to break out in a sweat.

Don't cry; don't cry; don't cry.

He hears the voice in his head, but it takes him a moment to place it. It belongs to a small child; one he hasn't heard in years. It's the voice of Flynae when she was four years old and they had first become mind-linked.

Don't you dare cry, is the response to the small child. This sounds like Flynae's current voice but much more stern than he has ever heard.

I won't! the child shouts back sounding as if she is crying already.

Remember who you are, the stern Flynae responds.

Kovad feels pain across his palm. He looks down to see his hand clenched and knows that Flynae's hand is in a fist tight enough that her claws drew blood.

A sign above a double door says exit. He hurries through it into the fading light outside.

The Emperor and Flynae are just now boarding Seko's shuttle. Lord Thyde knows that his isn't far. He begins sprinting.

Seko has pulled Flynae onto his lap again. "I've wined and dined you, my dear. Now it's time for you to put out." He grabs the front of her dress and begins ripping it.

I can't do this, the child screams.

Not a single tear, the stern voice yells.

Then a tone that he is more familiar with calls out to him. *Kovad. I need you.*

I know. I'm coming. He reaches out and pulls more energy to run faster. He feels the lump in her throat, the tension in her stomach, the dread overwhelming her.

He gives his shuttle verbal instructions through his wrist comm to start and set the autopilot destination for his command ship. By the time he steps aboard, all he has left to do is make his way to the cockpit and strap himself in. The shuttle begins to lift off, and he retreats into his mind to look for her.

As he journeys through the dark to find her, he begins casting the landscape, getting it ready to take her back to it. Trees. Meadow. Twilight. A fading skyline. Fresh, sweet air. Delicate grass to kiss her bare toes. Soft music in the background.

As he gets close, a dim light appears in the distance. He

hurries towards it. The scene he stumbles upon surprises him.

Four-year-old Flynae is on the floor of her basement room. Her eyes are red with unshed tears. She's cowering under the glare of present-day Flynae standing over her, warning her not to cry.

Hey, he calls out softly.

Both heads turn towards him.

I'm here. He kneels and opens his arms.

The two morph into one, a perfect blend of each broken part; and she runs to him. He swoops her up and carries her to the place he prepared. She clings to his neck, her body trembling violently.

He takes a deep breath to control his rage, and she breathes with him to calm herself. He wants nothing more than to apologize over and over for his role in placing her in this situation, but now is not the time to be indulgent. Right now is about being present for her.

When he reaches the meadow, he sits on the ground and holds her. Her body jerks. He feels her attention slipping away.

Stay here. Stay with me. He gently turns her face to his.

Show me something you love. She needs a distraction to keep her from returning to her body.

He steadies himself and his attention on remaining with her. When he knows he has full control, he opens his physical eyes and slows his shuttle. The blur of the stars stops, replaced by individual twinkling orbs. She looks out his eyes with him into the magnificence of space.

It's amazing, she whispers.

He squeezes her in response. They stay like that for hours. The autopilot guides the shuttle into the hanger bay of his warship, but he doesn't get up.

Her body bucks in his arms, and her consciousness threatens to return to reality.

No. Don't go back.

Show me something else.

He imagines a blanket on the ground in front of them and lays down, holding her delicate frame close against him. The meadow in front of them becomes a small pond with a waterfall at one end.

That's on Halaa, she whispers, recognizing the scenery as being a half an hour's horse ride from Cellyna's ranch.

Yes.

You've been swimming there, too, haven't you?

Yes. He knew she liked knowing there was a place that they had both been and enjoyed.

She grips his arm and closes her eyes. Only once he knew she was asleep did he allow himself to doze off.

41

Prepared (Flynae)

Flynae wakes up shivering even though the floor is heated. The warmth can't make up for her nakedness and the shock shaking her body. Every inch of her is sore.

Her breath comes quick and shallow as she first notices the additional bite marks on her arms. With a great effort, she sits up and leans against the nearby bed. She strains her ears to hear if anyone is around. When her breath and heartbeat are the only nearby sounds, besides the low rumbling vibration of the ship moving through space, she lets down her guard and begins weeping. At first, hot tears well up in her eyes and sting their way down her cheeks. Her body begins hitching with uncontrollable sobs.

Through her greatly blurred vision, she sees that her breasts, stomach, and thighs are also covered in angry red bites with blue halos. Some of them have broken skin while others are mostly bruises. Pain in the lowest part of her torso leads her to believe that she was not only raped but also sodomized.

Grabbing a sheet from the bed to cover herself with, she curls into a ball on the floor and cries.

Flynae. He reaches out tentatively, wanting her to know he's available.

She presses the sheet to her eyes and holds her breath to stop her sounds, unwilling to cry in front of him even in their minds. *I need a few minutes.*

This torments him; she can feel it, knowing that he wants nothing more than to be her comfort.

Just a few minutes. Please. Her throat tightens.

He wars with himself, wanting to push her to stop hiding her pain from him, while equally vowing to never force her to do anything she doesn't want to do. *I'm close if you need me.*

He directs his attention away, but she can't fully allow herself to break down again, knowing that he is on full alert to return to her.

Flynae's not alone for long before the two Kaliah enter the room. She cringes.

Their faces betray no emotions. Even their scents are hard and stone-like as if they have learned over the centuries how to reveal nothing.

They help her to her feet and lead her back to the room with the giant tub. Hot water is poured, and she is washed again with sweet-smelling salts and oils. Once she is out and dry, the upper half of her hair is pulled back and braided. Another human disguise is cast on her, concealing her eyes, ears, and the bruises.

Something sharp stabs her upper arm. As she turns to witness a needle being pulled from her, her other arm is assaulted with a second injection.

The room spins.

Flynae struggles to remain upright as the women dress her

in a tight corset, stockings, and a garter belt.

Her heart races as she realizes she is being prepared for someone again. Does the Emperor require her to be dolled up again? An off-the-shoulder, bohemian-style dress is put on over the lingerie. The low neckline shows off the small swells of her breasts pushed up by the tight corset. The long sleeves have slits from the wrists to the neckline. The skirt has an asymmetrical hem that comes up to her hip on one side.

Once she is deemed ready, they fasten a floor-length cloak around her shoulders and walk her from the room. Whatever they injected her with slows all her reactions and motor skills. She has to lean onto the women leading her to remain upright, as she wonders what new torment she is being led to.

The women accompany her to a shuttle where they place her in a seat and leave her. The pilot and co-pilot are human. Under other conditions, she might have had the ability to overpower them and take the ship, but whatever they gave her is strong. In her current condition, she can't even stand on her own.

The flight doesn't last for long, but the motion of the shuttle landing brings with it fresh terror. What could be waiting for her? The vibration beneath her tells her that she is still in space aboard another large ship.

Two human guards come aboard and pull her to her feet. She stares at the large grey, steel landing bay and wonders where she's seen it before. Even her perfect memory has succumbed to the effects of the drug.

Her panic rises as they lead her down strange yet familiar corridors. Breathing comes with great difficulty, and she begins hyperventilating.

Flynae, it's okay.

Crush you! She instantly feels bad for her outburst, but she has no more control over her thoughts than she does her breath at this point. *How can you say that anything is okay right now?* She recognizes that she wasn't prepared for the Emperor again this evening; he was sending her to someone else like she was no more than a common whore.

Because you're aboard my ship right now. He's sending you to me.

42

The Gift (Kovad)

Lord Thyde takes a moment to calm his elevated heart rate and collect himself before getting up from his desk to meet her in the hallway. After only a few steps, he pauses and stops at the doorway when her heart begins racing even more at the sound of his footsteps. The grey corridor in front of her morphs into a warped metal scene of the street where her father was murdered. His hand clenches into a fist as he works to calm his anger and frustration. All he wants is to go comfort her, but he can't walk to her without causing her to relive a nightmare.

Her mind conjures a twisted image of him walking down the hall towards her, a lifesword in his raised hand. Panic spurs her to react instinctually, and she struggles against the guards holding her. They've underestimated her physical abilities since she's half the size of either of them, and she slips from both their grips only to fall to the floor. Agony sets every nerve in her body on fire and immobilizes her.

"Enough," Lord Thyde shouts down the hallway, advancing towards Flynae and her escorts. He can't help her reaction and won't allow the guards to touch her again.

The soldier who had used the stun gun on her drops it in surprise, stands up, backs away, and snaps to attention.

Flynae curls into a ball, her hands coming up to her ears as if that will stop her from hearing his footfalls.

Kovad stops a few feet away. "What is the meaning of this?" he demands of the guards.

One of the men clears his throat before answering. "The Emperor sends you a gift for the evening, my lord. He says he'll send to collect her in the morning."

"Received. Dismissed."

The men salute him with a fist over their hearts before turning to march away.

Once they're out of sight, he drops to a knee next to her. "Flynae," he says softly. He wants to scoop her up in his arms and hold her tightly but resists not knowing how she will react.

Her hands press tighter to her head, her arms shaking under the strain. *This is an evil trick. It must be whatever they gave me.*

It's real. I'm here.

Flynae inhales and relaxes slightly, recognizing his scent. She opens her eyes and pushes up until she's sitting on her hip, looking at him. Everything revolves and contorts around her like the worst carnival ride ever. When she closes her eyes, the vibrations of the spaceship shake her. They're exaggerated and rocking like a boat on stormy seas. Finally, her gaze returns to him again.

He reaches for her, wanting to help; but she recoils and puts a hand out between them in a warding gesture.

"I can walk." She looks at the floor and sees in her mind the steps that are needed for her to stand, but her legs don't want to cooperate. *If I can get up*. She huffs in frustration as her body fails her. *Crush me! I'm just a pile of mush.* Helplessness threatens to overwhelm her.

Lord Thyde moves his hand, palm up, to the periphery of her vision. She sees it, sighs, and then places her hand in his.

He resists the urge to grasp it as tightly as possible so that no one can ever take her away and begins lifting her. When her other hand flails, he grabs it as well.

When she is on her feet, her body now inches from his, she backs away until she bumps the wall behind her, her gaze on his boots.

Kovad refuses to be offended by her actions and settles on confusion as he searches her mind for her motivation. Her thoughts reveal that she's barely holding herself together and is worried that she'll break down if she allows herself to receive any of his comfort.

"It's not far. And then you can rest." He doesn't touch her but holds his arms at the ready in case she stumbles.

She nods and focuses on putting one foot in front of the other.

43

Disguise (Kovad)

Once they're inside, Lord Thyde closes the door and hurries to wheel over his desk chair for her. "Sit," he says softly.

Thinking only of the relief of being off her unsteady legs, she allows herself to fall into the chair and close her eyes. After a breath, she says, "This is your chair."

"Yes." He kneels so that he isn't standing over her.

"It smells like you."

He chuckles. "Don't I smell like me?"

She nods. "Yes. But the chair smells more like...neutral you. You smell–." She pauses to breathe in again. "Conflicted."

"That's fair." He's overly aware of his every pulse, every breath, every motion, being this close to her. She's like a magnet, pulling him in; and he needs to resist.

Flynae finally opens her eyes and meets his, but he doesn't like knowing her real eyes are hidden from him behind a disguise.

"How do we remove this?" His mind seamlessly fills in what he didn't verbalize.

"Hmm." She looks at the energy of it, mingled with her own. It feels like a brick wall energetically cutting her off from her surroundings. She bangs on the mental image of it but can't even make it vibrate. *I can't do anything with it. The casters are more skilled than I am.* She leans her head back, exhausted and dizzy by the slightest exertion.

Using her aura as a compass, he finds his way to the other side of the wall of energy. There is no way either of them would individually be able to bring it down.

Without prior thought, he takes her hand. She gasps at his touch and the explosion of power that ignites. The barrier tumbles down, and he's staring into her feline eyes. They're both momentarily stunned by what just happened. It was like their abilities did more than combine; they multiplied together exponentially.

She sees herself, staring back at him, her ears standing tall beside her head, her arms and legs covered with blue and purple bites. She recoils and covers her face with her hands, disturbed by her battered body, but that doesn't stop her from seeing it through his eyes.

Hot rage floods through his being. He can't believe anyone could be so cruel to her.

The acrid scent of his wrath assaults her nose, and she leans away.

Knowing that he has lost control of his emotions, he stands and walks to the other side of the room, clenching and unclenching his fists. Every time he thinks he regained his composure, the anger returns just as strong. As a brief distraction, he speaks into his comm to one of his generals. "Bring me antiseptic ointment, arnica, water, chicken broth, and two raw eggs."

"Yes, my lord." The general doesn't hesitate nor question.

After another moment, Lord Thyde returns to Flynae's side. He sees her struggling to get a full breath against the confines of the corset. "Let's get that vile thing off you." He speaks as gently as he can, not wanting to traumatize her further. "Lean forward for me? Please?" He phrases it as a request, wanting her to know that she had the right to refuse.

She sees what he has planned and holds onto the front of her dress while resting against the arm of the chair. He reaches down the back of her dress and pulls the laces completely off the corset. Once they're removed, he's able to pull it up and out.

"Thank you," she whispers.

"How else can I make you more comfortable?"

Her thoughts automatically flash to the garter belt and stockings that she abhors, and her cheeks burn red at the thought of what it would require for him to take them off.

"The blouse is loose. I can unfasten the belt from the back." Once more, he leaves it as an option rather than an order.

She holds the front neckline in place again while allowing him to reach down the back of her dress. She involuntarily stiffens away from his touch on her skin as he unhooks the garter.

Kovad kneels in front of her. "Will you let me take off the nylons."

She imagines the feel of his hands running up her legs, under the skirt, to her thighs. Would he resist moving them further? She wouldn't be able to stop him in her current condition if he wanted to take advantage of her.

He places his hands on her knees and shakes her gently. "You aren't an object or a toy to be used. I would never–."

Her body hitches, and she hides her face in her hands.

44

The Child (Kovad)

Since she's physically shutting him out, he goes to her in her mind. Flynae sits on the floor of her room, appearing as a small child, hugging her legs, making herself as minuscule as possible.

Kovad sits down across from her. *What do you need right now?*

I can't–. It's all too much. If I let my guard down, even just a little, I won't be able to stop myself from crying.

What's so wrong with that?

The child squeezes her eyelids shut before looking at him. *I can't. You're a human.*

I hear you saying that you can't cry in front of a human, but you haven't told me why.

I don't even know. She pounds her fists on her thighs in frustration.

He scoots forwards until he can take her hand. *What is the worst that can happen?*

I haven't the faintest idea.

Do you trust me?

I do. The response is absolute and without hesitation.

He holds open his arms. *Well then. Let's face it together.*

The child climbs into his arms and begins to sob.

His most painful memories come rushing in blocking out all other thoughts. In one moment, he is ten and consoling his mother after fighting off the attackers that had broken in. In a blink, he's a few years older and with his mother again as they watch the news that his father's ship exploded in space. Another blip and he's with Cellyna shortly after they were married. She's nursing him back to health after the Emperor whipped him. Next flash. He's deciding to leave Cellyna so that he doesn't hurt her further.

All these memories come in like a great flood of pain, grief, and regret. The combination of them all at once threatens to bring tears to his eyes.

That is until he notices the pain diminishing. It was just the slightest amount, but enough that he realizes something is happening to the memories.

He blinks and notices the child in his arms. Her face is twisted in pain. The faintest shimmering trail runs from him into her. Her agony grows greater with every moment that he's aware of the pain of his past.

An awareness solidifies into knowing. Kaliah tears heal human hurts. She's absorbing the sorrow from his memories.

With much effort, he focuses on her and pushes his past behind him. It remains, like a great weight, a giant boulder he's shouldering and preventing from landing on her, ready to fall on them both if he lets down his guard.

He looks up at Flynae, sitting in his computer chair watching him. A solitary tear has escaped her.

"I've got it. You're safe," he whispers

She only hesitates a moment before pushing herself out of

the chair and falling into his arms.

Kovad holds her tightly as she weeps and allows all the barriers she has so carefully maintained to fall.

When his wrist comm makes a beep, she jerks.

He squeezes her. "It's okay. It's just the things I sent for." He stands and sets her in the chair before answering the door. After taking the tray and dismissing the soldier, he turns to see her hands over her ears again trying to drown out the noise of his steps.

He frowns as he pauses to think and kicks off his boots before padding back over to her in his socks. "Better?" He's rewarded with a smile that makes his entire body light up.

"Remarkably. Thank you."

He sets the tray down on his desk. "Eggs or broth?"

"Water?" The drug has left her with some terrible dry mouth. Everything is still spinning, but not as bad as it was when she was completely on edge and guarded.

Kovad hands her the glass and helps her when he sees how unsteady her hands are.

"How many of these are you going to let me treat?" He looks at the marks on her arms.

She thinks about all the places on her body that are bitten and bruised. "Some?"

"I'll take it," he says with a deep exhale. "Are you going to be more uncomfortable if I move you to my bed? I don't have a second chair here. I can send for one if you would rather."

"I'll be fine if you tell me you won't hurt me." She knows it, but she needs to hear it from his mouth.

He kneels next to her and takes her hand. "I'll be spending the rest of my life doing my human best to never hurt you again."

"That's enough for me." The edges of her mouth twitch with a shy smile.

Lord Thyde helps her stand and then lifts her off her feet. She puts her arms around his neck. He can't resist with her so close and presses his cheek against the top of her head.

When a tear escapes down her face, he's prepared and pushes away the painful past that threatens to ruin the moment. His focus remains on her.

45

Sleep (Kovad)

Setting her down takes a minute as Kovad has to convince his arms to release her. He goes back out for the tray and places that on the end table before sitting next to her. With the most gentle of touches, he starts addressing the wounds on her arms and shoulders.

Every few moments, he needs to take a few extra breaths or pause to calm his growing rage. He wants to unleash it on something. It continues to grow every time he realizes that he's helpless to prevent it from happening again. To distract himself, he focuses on checking in with her and making sure she feels comfortable.

The neckline of the dress falls across an angry bite bruise, and she keeps pulling it away.

"One of my button-down shirts would probably be as long as a dress on you. Does that sound more comf–"

"Yes." Flynae couldn't stop herself from interrupting with the thought of being wrapped up in his smell. She covers her open mouth with her hand as her cheeks turn an endearing shade of pink.

"I'll be right back." From his closet, he retrieves a black shirt. He helps her into it and buttons it down her front.

Rewarding him with a heart-warming grin, she holds out her arms; the sleeves continue for about six inches past her hands. He rolls them up for her with a smile.

She reaches up under the shirt and pulls the dress down. Getting it past her hips is a little bit of a struggle. Once it's halfway down her thighs, she accepts his help removing it and the stockings the rest of the way. The movement exhausts her, and she drops her upper back and head against the headboard.

Kovad exhales roughly as he gets a clear look at her bruised legs. She brings the sleeve of his shirt up to her nose.

"Neutral me?"

She nods.

He runs a hand over his forehead and through his hair. Nothing eases the torrent of tormenting emotions he's holding back. As a distraction, he sets to work methodically treating the marks on her legs.

Painful memories begin snaking their way into his mind: standing above four-year-old Flynae as she weeps over the body of her father, Cellyna begging him not to return to work and space so soon, his mother keeping herself composed for the cameras at his father's funeral.

He begins to wonder why these thoughts have flooded in and sidetracked him when he recognizes the emotion and looks at Flynae. She's wiping a tear from her eye.

"Sorry." She sniffs. "I got overwhelmed. And since I'd already cried in front of you once, it was much harder to keep it back."

"It's okay." He sets the ointment aside since he'd attended to everything besides what was on her torso and upper thighs and moves next to her, pulling her into his arms. "It's safe to cry."

This was all the permission she needed to give in again.

He finds that it's easier to keep his torments at bay if he focuses on her: her hair, her skin, the feel of her body in his arms. He doesn't want to ever let her go.

Finally, she stops shaking with sobs and is still. After a moment, she stifles a yawn.

"You're safe to sleep. I'll stay with you until you do." He plans to let her sleep in the bed, and he'll sleep on his meditation mat in the adjoining room.

Her hand reaches out and grips his arm as her pulse increases. "Only until I sleep?" He's the only thing keeping her fear at bay.

His arms tighten around her. "I won't leave if you don't want me to. I'll hold you all night long."

46

Will (Flynae)

"Shh. Shh." The sound of her skates on the ice sings to her like a soothing lullaby. It's a crisp, clear sound that conjures images of freshly fallen snow. She can almost smell the clean air of a winter's day. The sound of the ice feels as cleansing as snow to her soul.

A strong hand grabs her waist. Their bodies are close as they spin together. She misses a hand connection into a lift and ends up falling on her butt. Instead of getting up and reacting, she allows her torso to lie back onto the ice.

Will's shadow falls over her. She opens her eyes and peers up at him.

"That's not the next move," he says flatly.

"So I made a mistake." She shrugs and doesn't move.

"You don't make mistakes."

She closes her eyes and appreciates the soothing cool of the ice on the back of her head. *If I lay here long enough, will I freeze to death?* Of course, no one would let her lay here for that long even if she wanted to.

She'd spent Friday night being wined, dined, and violated

by the Emperor. Saturday night was spent in Lord Thyde's comforting arms. On Sunday, she had been returned home and spent the night worried that Eksar was going to take advantage of her presence. Thankfully, he hadn't even felt the need to speak to her. Sekara had been worried and asked tons of questions, but Flynae hadn't given her any answers.

Now it was Monday afternoon. She'd gone to school as expected of her and headed to the ice rink after, but she didn't know how she was supposed to just carry on with her life and act like everything was okay.

Nothing was okay.

Why had she been sent to the Emperor? Was he going to expect to see her again? How was she going to get answers? She relaxes, and the chill of the ice seeps through her clothing.

"Flynae?" Will skates in a circle around her. "What are you doing? What's going on?"

That is a loaded question, my friend. Who knows what is going on? Not I. "I'm sorry." She forces herself to acknowledge him. "I wasn't paying attention."

He extends his hand. "I've never seen you mess up. Except. That one time when you ended up in the hospital."

She feels Eksar's hand on her mouth again, his warm air in her face. She struggles to breathe. Before she fully gives in to the panic, she remembers how it felt to relax and cry in Lord Thyde's arms. That memory has been her biggest source of comfort during the last thirty-six hours. She's replayed moments of it over and over again.

"I was just.... Hmm. Lost." She reaches out and takes his hand, allowing him to pull her to her feet.

He doesn't let go once she is upright. "Flynae, I'm worried about you."

She fights the urge to yank her hand back. It's not his fault that she can't handle being touched. His smell is one of concern and infatuation. *Oh, gods. He thinks he can save me,* she thinks right before he speaks again.

"Let's run away together."

She looks away, struggling with the urge to both laugh and cry with hysteria. *He has no clue what he is suggesting. Eksar would hunt him down and slay him.* "Will." She can't get more than his name out. How does she explain to him that she cares for him like a brother when she knows that he wants to be more. She never wanted to hurt him, but now that isn't an option.

Will begins moving closer. "I want to take care of you, Flynae. I know someone is hurting you, and I can't stand to see that anymore."

Her throat tightens like someone is gripping it. "Will. You're amazing." The tension continues down her throat into her chest and gut. She tries to pull her hand from his, but he tightens his grip. She moves backward, keeping the distance between them.

"And I care about you." She begins using her other hand to pull his off hers. "Will, let me go." Her pulse begins racing, and she starts to sweat. If he doesn't let go of her soon, she might be unable to stop herself from screaming. As much as he doesn't mean to, he's behaving like the other men who have forced themselves on her.

"Flynae." Her name comes out of his lips like a plea.

She begins to tremble as she knows what is coming next. She hears the words before he even speaks them. "Will, don't." This was only going to end in heartache now.

"I love you."

Even though she knew it was coming, she's as stunned as if

he had slapped her. She stares at him without blinking. He'd been wanting to say it to her for months now. She'd sensed it, smelled it. Now the words were sitting there in the air between them. If only she could open up his mouth and put them back inside. Instead, she has guilt for causing and not sharing his sentiment.

"I know." Her tone sounds cold, flat. She knows she can't show emotion or weakness now. It would only encourage him. "But you shouldn't. You can't."

"I can't help it."

She has to admit to herself that it isn't his fault. She was stupid for thinking she could ever be just friends with a human. This was her responsibility to avoid.

"I'm sorry." She wants to hang her head, but she refuses. She is a royal daughter and will carry herself as such even when she thinks she is undeserving. That is a duty she carries because of her blood. When she pulls her hand again, he releases it. She skates away and rushes to the locker room.

Hoping that he'll be gone by the time she comes out, Flynae takes her time changing. He is waiting by the exit rather. His skates sit on the floor at his side, but he's still wearing his skating clothes.

She looks straight ahead instead of meeting his eyes. When he stands in her way, she tries to go around him; but he moves to block her again.

She finds herself up against the wall with him in front of her. Not wanting to do something she'll regret, she takes a moment to breathe rather than give in to being frustrated.

She's staring at the wall, paying attention to inhaling into her diaphragm when Will leans down and kisses her. She controls her instinct to slap him having promised herself she would never do that again. Instead, she pushes him, harder than she meant to, and he falls backward.

"Crush you, Will." She storms out as quickly as she can without running.

"Flynae," he calls as he gets to his feet. "I'm sorry. I shouldn't have." He runs after her. "Please forgive me."

Her stomach knots. In a purely innocent way, he has become someone who takes from her without permission.

As she walks out the front doors, Will follows right behind.

"I'll see you tomorrow, right?" he asks, fear apparent in his voice.

"I don't know," she responds. It would be easier for both of them if she just disappeared. He needs space and time to move on.

"Flynae. Please!" he begs.

"Goodbye, Will," she says just loud enough for him to hear. Then she turns and runs away. As soon as she is out of sight, her tears start to flow.

47

The Gym (Flynae)

She feels Lord Thyde's focus on her as she slides another twenty-five-pound weight plate to each side of the bar. She doesn't secure the plates on the bar in case the weight proves to be too much, and she needs to dump it.

The gym is her refuge this week. She'd skipped all classes that would cause her to come into contact with Will and made her way to the gym rather than the ice rink each day after school. Lifting weights is not a substitute for gliding across the ice, but the physical activity was a helpful distraction. Today, she's trying to find out what her one-rep max for a chest press is.

Most of the other people around the weight floor are beefy men in muscle shirts. Several of them have stopped to watch the petite little girl who has enough weight on the bar to put some of them to shame.

Flynae ignores them, not even sparing a glance in their direction. When she had first come in, some of them had thought about asking her if she wanted help, but she had her best "stay-away" energy working. No one dared to get close.

She slides onto the bench and under the bar, feeling their eyes crawl along her skin. Her focus moves to the bar. She lifts it from the rests, lowers the bar until it grazes her chest, and then pushes it up and away. Her muscles strain, and she knows she's nearing her limit. She lowers the bar again and finds her arms beginning to shake as she arches her back to push it up.

Just as she is ready to give up and dump the weights, she hears him say, "You've got this. Just a little more."

Her eyes flutter from looking at the bar to finding Lord Thyde standing close, watching.

"What?" Her arms start to give out in her surprise. He rushes to grab the middle of the bar and helps her put it back on the stand.

Flynae sits up and sees the room is empty except for the two of them. "Hi." She smiles, and her face and ears burn.

"I thought you might need a little company after being alone all week." He's dressed in black track pants and a sleeveless black t-shirt that shows off his muscular chest, arms, and shoulders. She can't stop her eyes from taking him in, and it causes her to flush even further.

Finally, she gets herself under control and meets his eyes. "That is very kind of you." If she was being honest with herself, it had been a horrible week. She kept wondering if Will was okay. To keep the break clean, she'd cut off all contact and left his messages unread.

The two of them had a shared music playlist that they would add songs to that they wanted the other to hear. Since Will wouldn't know either way, she had kept up with the new music he had added during the week. They'd all been songs about heartbreak and loss, which only reinforced to her that she had made the right decision. The boy was way too attached to her if the songs came close to reflecting how he felt.

"I'm very impressed." Lord Thyde glances at the loaded bar she had recently lifted.

"Thank you. You going to give it a go?" She raises her eyebrows in challenge.

"All right. I'm not sure how I should feel about myself if you end up being able to lift more than I can."

Flynae moves out of the way, and he lays down on the bench. She finds herself watching his every move, admiring his physique. Flutters fill her from throat to stomach. She recognizes the emotion and feels a sense of disgrace. There is no way to deny that she is attracted to a human. Her father would be ashamed of her.

"Is that a Kaliah trait?"

His voice brings her out of her humiliating thoughts. "Huh?"

"Your superhuman strength?" He grabs the bar and begins lowering it.

"I guess so." Superhuman isn't enough though. It won't stop Eksar nor the Emperor from taking her when they want.

She shakes her head and brings herself back to the present, not wanting to miss another moment of being in Lord Thyde's presence.

48

Promise (Flynae)

The two of them lift weights together for another hour. With Lord Thyde's understated encouragement, she breaks a few personal records. He doesn't hide his astonishment, and she basks in his awe.

"You up for a little sparring?" He asks when she isn't certain what to do next.

Flynae's stomach jumps into her throat, and she struggles to swallow before responding. "I would love to."

He walks next to her as they move from the weight room to one more open and uncluttered.

Her body tingles at how close he is. She's never craved being near someone like this. All she wants is for him to hold her again. That was the safest she'd felt in a long time.

After scolding herself for thinking like a giddy schoolgirl, she widened the distance between them the tiniest bit. Accepting his comfort and encouraging his affection towards her only put him in danger.

When they stop, he wraps her hands. She watches his hands as he touches hers and wishes he would never let go. Air comes with difficulty as her inner conflict continues. He shouldn't even be here with her. There was no way that it was going to end well for them.

Kovad holds up some focus mitts. "Ready?"

Her eyes widen. "You want me to hit you?"

He laughs. "You aren't exactly hitting me. But, yes. Let's see what you've got."

She knows how to stand having seen people do this before. Not knowing how much force to put behind them, her first few strikes are tentative.

"Good." He nods. "Now stop holding back."

She doesn't need much more encouragement. Her next few punches get progressively more aggressive. After a solid hit, Lord Thyde has to recenter himself.

His eyes light up with approval. "Well done. Keep going."

While maintaining her form, she starts striking faster and faster. The endorphins flooding her body from the physical activity feels amazing. The focus mitts blur before her into a substitute for Eksar's face. She imagines hitting him again and again. Her arms fly faster. As her pace becomes more frenzied, her form suffers.

Lord Thyde says her name but she barely hears. Tears threaten her eyes. He steps aside, and she flails forward.

Kovad catches her around her waist; and energy explodes around them in a burst, an amplifying of the resources available to them. The building's lights blink, and the air unit stalls for a moment.

She jerks away and stares at him. "By the gods, what was that?"

"That was amazing." He can't hide the desire in his eyes to experience the feeling again.

Flynae trembles. For a brief moment, they had shared more power than anyone living had ever felt. She was certain of this and takes a step back.

He holds out his hand. "Don't you want to see if it will happen again?"

She shakes her head. "I don't." She knows how much he desires authority. His perseverance and willingness to push himself to his limits were most of how he had gained the Emperor's favor so quickly. Knowing as much as she does about human nature, she imagines that even he could be corrupted by wielding such cosmic energy. Her heart pounds in her ears.

"Hey, it's okay." He holds out his arms, palms up. When she doesn't retreat from him, he takes her trembling hands and begins unwrapping them. "I will never force you to do anything."

She meets his eyes with unwavering determination as she realizes that he has become the person whose betrayal would hurt her the most. It's an overwhelming feeling knowing that a human has such power over her.

He runs his thumbs over the backs of her hands setting her skin on fire beneath his touch before releasing them. "May I walk you home?"

Home. The word sends her body into a ball of knots. They both know she has no choice but to return there each night though she wonders what would happen if she didn't. Her fear is that the repercussions would be dealt to Senice or Fennec. She won't allow that to happen.

"I was going to shower here, first." Her voice comes out shakier than she intended. Whenever possible, she would shower at school or the ice rink. It allowed her to enjoy the water rather than strain her ears for any sound of Eksar approaching.

"A shower it is then." He walks with her until their paths fork for the respective locker areas.

As she begins peeling off her drenched shirt and sports bra, the mind link makes it seem as if he is in the room with her and able to see her bare skin. She closes her eyes, but that only allows her to see even more clearly through his as he undresses as well.

He steps into the shower first, and she can feel the warm water hitting his skin. As she washes, she can feel his hands moving over his body and knows the reverse situation is true for him as well. She takes a few deep breaths to collect herself and then begins to move just a little bit faster.

He waits for her in the hallway. She was determined to look unaffected by the shower experience, but she can feel her cheeks turning pink when he looks at her.

"May I?" He holds out his arm for her.

"Thank you." She loops hers around his. The lights flicker as their energies combine and magnify. The effect is more subdued than it had been earlier. She doesn't flinch from it this time.

They walk down suburban streets together, both of them contributing to a bubble of energy that would stop any human passing by from noticing them.

It's dark outside, and a myriad of stars light up the sky despite the nearby city lights. When she gazes up, he takes a moment to close his eyes and look through hers. Her Kaliah eyes can see three times as many stars as his human ones.

Are you going to remember that view the next time I need a distraction? She hadn't meant to ruin the moment and mention her fear, but it was getting more difficult to not think about Eksar the closer they got to his house.

Dread creeps over her as she sees a vision of herself on the basement floor. In her mind, a boot connects with her stomach. Her body responds as if it were real. She bends at the waist as the wind is knocked from her lungs. She might have fallen to her knees had she not been holding Lord Thyde's arm. He grabs her around her waist until she gets her feet back.

"What was that?" It's a question that doesn't need an answer; they both know it was a vision of something to come.

Even as her terror heightens to the point that she wants to curl into a ball and cry, she straightens herself, pulls her shoulders back, and steps back to meet his eyes.

"No matter what happens tonight, promise me you won't intercede."

He tightens his jaw and clenches his left fist. "Flynae. I can't-"

"There is no can't in this, Lord Thyde." Her voice is full of authority and sternness. "I'm fully aware of the strength of those who would defend me. And it isn't currently half of what it would be up against. You are a very clever strategist, my lord. You would not subject your forces to such a scenario. You would bide your time, would you not?"

He finds himself in awe of her, her strength, and her commanding presence. She's never looked so regal as she does in the current moment. "You are correct, my lady."

"Then we must wait. Will you promise me?"

He thinks back to the power they had generated together in the gym.

"Neither of us knows what that was. Would you risk everything with a strategy you don't know how to control or reproduce?"

"I would not."

"Then will you swear?"

It pains him to answer her, but he knows she is right. The words catch in his throat, but he forces himself to say them. "I promise, my lady."

"I should continue the rest of the way by myself. Eksar will already smell you on me. He doesn't need to know that you were nearby. Thank you for the company tonight, Lord Thyde. And for walking me home. I had a pleasant evening." She inclines her head briefly.

"The pleasure was all mine, Princess Let."

Knowing that her determination would only weaken with hesitation, she turns and walks away.

49

Basement (Kovad)

Watching her walk away now is one of the hardest things Lord Thyde has ever done. Flynae holds her head high though she knows exactly what she's walking into. He can see both the strong, regal warrior and the small, fragile child that she is. Everything in him wants to hold her and never let her go. She rounds the corner and is out of sight. He watches her through the mind link now.

He's never felt so helpless and it makes him angry. How is there nothing he can do to protect her? If he thought he had any chance at making a difference, he would stand between her and this fate.

Flynae enters the house and energetically scans it for any sign of Eksar without finding anything. That doesn't mean that he isn't in the basement. There is something about the basement that blocks the flow of energy. Neither of them knows how it is possible.

She makes her way downstairs and finds Eksar sitting on her bed as she enters her room. Lord Thyde's pulse quickens as much as Flynae's does.

"Where have you been?" the Kaliah male asks with disapproval in his eyes.

Her fear becomes anger that she struggles to contain. "The gym."

Eksar takes a deep breath. "With Kovad Thyde?"

She hates the sound of Kovad's name coming from Eksar's mouth. "Yes."

"Curious." He sits there evaluating for a moment.

She shifts her weight uncomfortably.

Eksar rises and grabs one of her wrists.

She reacts without thinking and swings her free hand to punch him in the stomach. He takes a step back, stunned, the air knocked out of his lungs; but he keeps a firm hold on her wrist.

For a moment, Kovad considers rushing in.

Remember your promise, Flynae responds to his impulsive thought. *He doesn't have permission from his master to kill me.*

This is enough to stop him. He did swear, and he'll be no use to her dead. The Emperor has a purpose for her, and Eksar would suffer if he did something to interfere with that.

Eksar jerks her arm so that she is square to him and shoves both her shoulders, knocking her to the floor. As he stands over her, she tucks her legs in and extends them, kicking him solidly in the stomach, knocking him back against the wall.

She jumps up while he is down. Instead of running, she leaps on him with her mouth open, her fangs out. He puts up his arm, and she bites down on his forearm. He slams her head down on the cement floor, and she nearly blacks out.

Eksar gets up, and his foot connects with her stomach as she had foreseen minutes before.

Kovad loses the ability to know what is happening as Flynae

loses consciousness. The silence in his mind is deafening. With the energy around the basement unable to flow freely in and out, he has no way of knowing if she is alive or dead. He hasn't felt alone in ten years now, and the feeling is unendurable.

He would know if she was just asleep. Then he can see her dreams. Now there is an empty space where she usually resides within reach at any time of day.

Cold fingers grip his spine. The emotion running through him is one he's not used to. Fear. He's afraid that he's going to lose her tonight. She's going to die on a hard basement floor.

Minutes pass like hours. He doesn't move from his post down the street from the house. Come morning, Eksar will leave, and Lord Thyde plans to retrieve her body.

He paces. He rages. Why did he let her go home, especially when she knew something horrible was coming?

The sky begins to lighten around 5 am, but still, he must wait. Finally, around 7 am, both Sekara and Eksar leave the house. Kovad waits a few minutes longer until they both are out of range of feeling their energy, and then he goes in.

When he enters the basement, he can feel her energy hanging on like a flame no bigger than a candle that could be snuffed out by a slight breeze. The scene in the room hits him like a gut punch.

She's on the floor, naked from the waist down, dark red blood drying on her pale thighs. Her shirt is ripped open and hangs on her shoulders like a rag. Her torso is black and blue. A deep purple bruise colors her cheek near a split lip.

He grabs a blanket from her bed and kneels next to her, wrapping her up, and pulling her into his arms. Her body is cold and feels unnaturally weightless as he lifts her.

She moans and grimaces but doesn't wake.

"I've got you, Flynae," he whispers, holding her so close that his lips brush her forehead. "Stay with me." He begins pushing energy into her body, worried that she has lasted the night only to expire at any moment.

As he carries her from the basement, images of himself walking to her father with his lifesword in his hand flood his mind. She's aware enough to hear and react to his footfalls. He resists his urge to curse, as he doesn't want to do anything to disturb or startle her now.

As soon as he is upstairs, he sends a message on his comm with his location for his shuttle to pick him up. He takes her outside and stands with her face and wrapped body in the sun hoping that it will warm and comfort her. He sends a communication request to Senice next.

"Lord Thyde?" Senice sounds puzzled and curious. The only exchange that Lord Thyde and Senice have had in the last fourteen years was Flynae's first hospital emergency two years ago.

"Where do Kaliah go in Solum for emergency care?" Kovad is aware of and disappointed at how inept the humans were at caring for Flynae during her last trip to the hospital. If he can avoid that now, he will.

"The Albatross Hospital. It's on the east side. Ask for Dr. Lamb." After a brief breath, Senice asks, "Is it Flynae again?"

"Yes."

"I'm on my way." The comm ends.

Flynae coughs and a tiny bit of red foam bubbles out of her mouth onto her lips. He gently wipes it off and continues to channel more energy into her.

His shuttle lands in the street in front of them. He carries her aboard and sits in front of a heating vent with her as he directs the pilot to the Albatross. As they near the hospital, her body comes alive enough to begin shivering. He counts this as a good sign though it increases the pain in her ribs. There is a good chance some of them are broken.

He calls ahead, asking that Dr. Lamb meets them at the shuttle pad on the roof. As the shuttle touches down, she opens her eyes and looks at him. His whole body floods with joy and relief at the sight of her bright green eyes.

Kovad?

I'm here. I have you. Stay with me.

She tries to take a deep breath and grimaces.

I know it hurts. Don't struggle. It'll be better soon. He caresses her cheek, hoping that it will soothe her, and carries her out.

She's unconscious again by the time he's laying her on the waiting stretcher. He notices an energy mirage around one of the doctors and recognizes a disguised Kaliah.

"Dr. Lamb."

The doctor's eyes widen in recognition at the sight of Flynae. "She's a royal daughter."

"Yes."

"Who did this to her?"

Lord Thyde hesitates for only a moment before responding. She must be important to her people, and he wants all of them to know who is responsible. "Eksar Let."

The doctor pauses. He looks at Kovad gauging how serious he is. Then he turns to Flynae. "I've got her. She'll get the best of care. Does Senice know?"

"He's on his way."

Kovad stands there watching them wheel her away from him, knowing he can't accompany her into surgery.

50

Awake (Flynae)

Flynae feels like a crumbled heap of bricks as she begins to come to consciousness. The room smells sanitized, but not by harsh chemicals, and fresh like there is a living plant or two present. Music plays off to her right; she detects the rhythm of a heartbeat in the refrain. It takes her a moment to realize that it is playing her heartbeat.

Her left arm twitches as she tries to move it, but her hand seems stuck, enclosed. It jerks as she tries to free it. Something tightens around it. She yanks harder with her limited strength. Her eyes are still closed, but she senses someone sitting up nearby. They exhale.

She jerks again. The music on the machine next to her plays a little faster as her heart rate increases. The inability to move is maddening.

Lord Thyde's words cut through the panic. "Hey. You're okay." His hand tightens around hers, and he places his free hand on her shoulder, holding her down. "You shouldn't move." His voice is soft with care and heavy with fatigue.

Flynae opens her mouth to speak but can't make a sound.

Where–where–where? Her mind gets stuck on the single word like a skipping record.

"You're at the hospital. You're coming out of anesthesia. Try to relax."

Her body finally begins to respond to her demands, and her hand grips his. She opens her eyes.

They're in a room that is mostly dark except for a few soft lights along the floor. The walls are a warm caramel color. A potted tree sits near the closed window blinds.

"What happened?" She meets his gaze. "Why?" The last thing she remembers is lifting weights alone at the gym. Then he had surprised her, and–. His memories come flooding into her brain all at once. The emotions and events are overwhelming.

She squeezes her eyes shut and covers her face with her free hand as tears threaten. The pain of the events takes over as the anesthesia continues to wane. Her ribs feel like she is sideways in a vice. The ache between her legs confirms her deepest fears.

When she breaks down and begins sobbing, he leans over her, and she wraps her arm around his neck.

"Try to lie still," Kovad whispers, knowing how much pain the movements are causing. He resists the torrent of painful memories that threaten to distract him from her.

Gradually, she begins to get herself back under control. When he sits up, she sees his eyes have a sheen to them. She wipes her face dry.

"Everything okay in here?" a melodic voice asks from the doorway as an undisguised female Kaliah nurse comes in. She walks soundlessly to the bedside. "I heard the monitor speed up and thought I should check on you. Do you want a sedative?"

Flynae grips Lord Thyde's hand as she shakes her head no.

She wants to be able to move more not less.

The nurse reaches out her hand and holds it a few inches from Flynae's side, checking the energy there. "Your ribs are healing nicely. They'll be bruised and sore for a while, but the bones are almost knit back together. You'll have more mobility soon. Give them another few hours, okay?"

Flynae nods in response.

"How's the pain level? Do you need something for that?"

"No. I'm fine."

"Rest then. I'll be close by if you need anything." The nurse walks out as silently as she came.

Flynae turns to Lord Thyde. "Where did you hear about the Albatross?" Flynae was familiar with the hospital as all the Kaliah know what facilities are operated by their species in the city.

"From Senice."

Her stomach hardens like a stone as the horror of his words grips her. "You told him?" She dramatically throws her free arm over her face. "Gods."

"Yes. I had to. I didn't know where to take you, and I wasn't about to leave you in incompetent hands again."

She wanted to slip through the bed and disappear. If Senice knew where she was then he was probably going to find out about everything this time. That meant Fennec was going to know as well.

"He'll be here soon." The comm on his wrist vibrates slightly, and he glances down at it. "Or he's here now. They just landed."

A shiver runs through her.

"Are you cold?"

She sighs. "No. Just dread."

"Will it be easier for you if I stay or go?"

She looks at him and really sees him for the first time since waking. His normally bright eyes are dark with fatigue yet full of concern. "You haven't slept."

"I dozed a little." His thumb caresses the back of her hand.

"Go sleep. I'll be okay. I can face my family alone. I need-," her voice breaks with the threat of more tears. *I need you to be okay.* Her body quivers at the thought of him releasing her and leaving.

"I'll see you soon. You won't miss me for long."

"I miss you already."

"I know." He brings her fingertips to his lips before gently setting her hand down. "My lady," he says as he stands.

"My lord."

51

Family (Flynae)

She isn't alone for long, maybe a minute or two, before Fennec enters. He sees her and rushes to lay next to her on the bed being careful not to jostle her. She snuggles her head against his.

He takes a deep breath and lets it out; the warm air tickles her neck.

"Why do you smell like Lord Thyde?" he whispers.

"Umm." She bites her lower lip. Senice is the only one who knows about the mind-link.

"And why is he out in the hallway looking like he's running on fumes talking to Senice and Dr. Lamb?"

"Umm." She picks up Fennec's hand and interlaces her fingers into his. "Well." She stares at his hand and focuses on the comfort of the side of her head against his cheek. She didn't want to hear what they were discussing out in the hallway. It would be difficult enough when Senice talked to her about it. "Because he was just here."

Fennec chuckles. "Obviously. And for some time. The whole room smells like him." Fennec turns his head away and takes another sniff. "And he was definitely worried about you. Why would that be, little sister? How do you know one of the Emperor's henchmen?"

Flynae grimaces at the derogatory term. "Rude."

"It's only rude if you disagree."

Movement by the doorway causes them to turn in time to see Senice walk in. Flynae's heart hurts to see such sorrow on his beautiful face.

"Dear one," he greets her. She closes her eyes as he touches her face and kisses her forehead.

"Uncle, I'm sorry." She squeezes her eyes shut, but a few tears manage to sneak out under her closed lids.

He sits down next to her on the bed, his hip against hers, and takes her hand. "Whatever are you sorry for, dear one?"

"I was so afraid to tell you." Her whole body begins trembling. "I didn't want you to do something that would get you hurt. Or worse." She's aware that her strong emotions have attracted Lord Thyde's attention.

I didn't mean to intrude. I was just concerned.

You're never intruding. I have nothing to hide from you.

"Dear one." Senice pauses, his face creased with worry, and shakes his head. "You've done nothing wrong. I failed to protect you." His hand tightens on hers.

She smells Fennec's confusion, but he doesn't ask. He just snuggles even closer, providing her with comforting warmth.

"You aren't going back." Senice's tone is authoritative.

She opens her mouth to interject, but he holds up a finger, stopping her.

"Dr. Lamb advised that we give your ribs a couple more hours here to finish the healing process. I have Kaliah combing the area for Eksar. He doesn't seem to be on the planet. If I'm alerted of him approaching, we'll leave immediately, okay?"

She nods.

Fennec picks up his head at the mention of Eksar's name and looks from Flynae to Senice and back again. Flynae averts her gaze. Feeling and smelling their pain is already too much. She doesn't want to see it in their eyes.

They pass a few quiet hours waiting. Senice orders in food, but she finds it difficult to have more than a few bites.

Fennec regales her with a recap and update of all the animals waiting to see her on Halaa. There were some freshly hatched chickens and new baby pigs. Cellyna had recently gotten a puppy named Zelda because her other dog was getting old, and she couldn't stand the idea of being without a dog for even a day. No one had any idea what breed Zelda was. After a DNA test, they discovered the dog was no less than twenty-three breeds.

When she couldn't stifle a yawn, Senice encouraged her to sleep. Fennec cozied in next to her again, and she grips his hand.

52

The Monarch's Daughter (Flynae)

She wakes up to shadows congregated at the door to the room. Senice is there, quietly conversing with Dr. Lamb and the nurse.

Flynae hears the doctor say, "We are very disturbed by it." Her cheeks burn at her first guess at what they're talking about. She hates that they can look at her and know what happened.

Fennec brushes by them with a shopping bag in his hand and a grin on his face. "Are you ready for this, Flybaby?"

She openly yawns in front of her big brother and uses the control on the bed to sit up. "Whatcha got there, Fenn?"

"The softest. The most luxurious. The plushiest robe ever." He pulls the garment from the bag and tosses it at her face.

She pulls it in against her cheek appreciating how warm and velvety it feels. "Is this my outfit for getting out of here?"

"I got these, too." He pulls out a pair of loose linen pants and a t-shirt for her.

"They're perfect. Help me stand up." She swings her legs off the bed and pauses for a moment to catch her breath. The nurse wasn't kidding when she said Flynae would feel bruised for a while. Kaliah healers will use their abilities on deep, serious wounds but can't waste their energy on superficial injuries.

Fennec grabs her under her shoulders so as not to press on her bruises. "Where are we going?" he whispers conspiratorially, making her grin.

"You're helping me to the restroom where I can get changed in peace, by myself."

Fennec frowns and continues speaking in a low voice. "Are you sure this plan of yours is solid?"

"Absolutely not," she murmurs back at him. "But it's the only one I've got, and I need your help."

He grabs the clothing bag and supports her as she hobbles her way to privacy. "What if you fall?" he asks after helping her sit on the closed toilet lid.

"Turn around then. I just need a moment. And then you know I didn't fall." Once his back is turned, she shrugs the hospital gown off and slips the t-shirt on. It's a little more difficult for her to wriggle the pants on.

"Okay," she calls out. "I'm going to need help with the robe."

Fennec hurries to her side. As he ties the front around her waist, she sees an extra shine to his feline eyes.

"Fenn." Her throat tightens with the potential of tears. "Don't. Please."

"What did he do to you?"

Rather than watching her big brother cry, Flynae chooses to fall into his arms. "I'm okay, Fennec. I'm okay." Her voice sounds convincing enough, but she doesn't believe herself. She's barely staying sane. What will happen if she snaps, she wonders.

She holds onto him as he leads her back out.

"Are you ready?" Senice asks.

"Yeah. Let's blow this joint."

Fennec rewards her with a snort at her joke. She grins at him.

"They're all behind you, Flynae," Senice says.

"Who?" She looks out the doorway. Her vision is quickly cut off by a wall, but she senses multiple beings lined up just to the right. "What?" She backs up a step. "What's going on?"

"They just want to pay honor, dear one." Senice walks to her and takes her hands. He pulls some of the nervous energy from her and dissipates it. "You're Issiah's daughter."

Her chin levels at the sound of her father's name. She closes her eyes and sees the form of a man in black approaching him with a lifesword in hand. She refuses to see the face of the shadow in her mind.

Flynae takes a deep breath and looks down at herself. Fennec hasn't dressed her terribly. The robe hides her casual shirt and is royal emerald green in color. Her brother knew what he was doing.

Without further pause, she walks from the room. The hall is lined with a dozen Kaliah on each side. They incline their heads or bow as she passes by. Many of them breathe the word, "Highness."

She doesn't think and only focuses on putting one foot in front of the other and keeping her head up until they're in the elevator. As soon as the doors close, Senice and Fennec rush to support her.

"Why? Why were they calling me that?" Her head spins. She looks at Senice. "Isn't it you or Eksar?"

Her uncle shakes his head. "It's only one every generation, dear one."

"Then it's Siah, right? He's almost as old as you are."

"There's a chance it's not him."

53

Questions (Flynae)

"It's not me," she repeats as they board Senice's shuttle. She settles into a seat, draws her knees up, and hugs them to her chest.

Senice gives her a few minutes as he navigates the shuttle into space and activates lightspeed. Then he comes back and sits next to her. "Why do you say that, dear one?"

"Wouldn't I feel different? I'm not stronger than you by any stretch."

He laughs softly. "You have another hundred years or more to come into your full potency."

She throws her arms open for a moment in exasperation. "So if it is me, and I won't be strong enough until then, Eksar and Seko get to conspire and run unchecked for the next hundred years?"

Senice frowns. "Eksar *and* Seko?"

She covers her open mouth with her hand. "You didn't know?"

He shakes his head. "What are they doing?"

"I couldn't tell you exactly. I just know they're communicating. Trading favors." *Trading me as favors.* She shudders.

"Well, now we have three things we need to discuss. Are you up for it now?"

"Do you have wine?"

He smiles. "I always have wine."

Fennec jumps up from nearby. "I'll get it." He returns with three stemless glasses filled nearly to the brim.

Flynae crosses her legs and cups the glass in front of her with both hands. She inhales the dark red liquid appreciating its rich berry aromas before taking two quick sips. She closes her eyes and takes a deep breath before looking at her uncle. "Okay. I'm ready."

"Do you want to start with the difficult one or the easy one?" Senice's face tenses with emotional pain as he waits for her answer.

"There's an easy one? Oh, goodie. Let's start there." She takes another sip of wine followed by another deep inhale.

"Would you describe what happened between you and Lord Thyde at the gym, please?"

She brings her hand up over her face. "Oh, gods. Crush me. That's the easy one?" She feels both their eyes on her and smells Fennec's surprise.

"Yes," Senice says.

As she thinks back to the night at the gym, she feels water falling over her body and the sensation that felt like his hands on her skin and her hands on his. Her face and body begin to flush. She shakes her head. That couldn't be what Senice was asking about.

"What did he tell you?" So much happened that night, and it was all currently jumbled in her brain.

"That the two of you touched and the energy changed."

Her body tingles with the memory of that moment; it was simultaneously wonderful and frightening. Both emotions vie for prominence. The look on his face had been one of lust and desire. Tension grips her torso and shoulders, and then his arm around her waist, supporting her, making sure she didn't fall.

She swallows. "Yes." When her hands begin to tremble, she takes another sip.

Senice leans forward in his seat. "Can you tell me more about it?"

"I've never felt anything like it. It was like all the energy in the galaxy was there at my disposal. For a moment, I felt like I had the option to do anything. I could levitate or create a tornado if I wanted to. But not just destructive things. It felt like I could smash a plate into pieces no bigger than sand and put it back together as if it had never happened."

Senice and Fennec exchange a look. Fennec smirks.

"What? I know what you're both thinking." Her voice has a scolding tone now. "I'm not the Monarch. It has only happened when we've touched."

"Wait. It's happened more than once."

She groans and scrubs her face. "Twice. It's happened twice. The first wasn't as...intense."

"When was that?"

Her mind flashes back in time to being prepared for the Emperor the first night and Lord Thyde the second night. "Last week." So much had happened in just a short amount of time. She squeezes her eyes shut trying to keep the overwhelm from causing her to roll into a little ball.

"Hold up. How often do the two of you hang out?" Fennec asks with a creased forehead.

Every moment she has ever spent with Lord Thyde flashes through her mind: him murdering her father, him chasing away the bullies at school and her telling him to leave her alone, him coming to see her at the hospital, him carrying her away from the boys at the party, him kissing her hand at the banquet. They all flood in together.

She lets out an involuntary laugh. "Hang out?" She lifts her eyes to look at her bewildered brother. "I'd say once, Fenn. We've 'hung out' once." The night at the gym. She would count that as hanging out.

Fennec shakes his head. "I don't know what is happening here. When did this all start?"

In a calm voice, Flynae responds, "Well, that one time at band camp..."

The three of them share a much-needed laugh. As the sound of mirth fades, she feels like a small child again, kneeling next to her father's expiring body while Lord Thyde grabs her shoulder and lifts his lifesword.

"Hey." Fennec touches her knee, causing her to jump. "Come back to us."

She gives him a weak smile.

"Do you need a break?" Senice offers.

"From talking?" Flynae shakes her head and drains her glass. "The wound is still bleeding. Might as well dig out the bullet now."

Senice stands and holds out his hand for her glass. "More wine?"

"Most definitely."

Am I interrupting? Kovad's calming presence draws nearer.

You're awake. Hiding her emotions mentally is much more difficult than keeping them physically concealed. Excitement pervades her thoughts.

Yes. I just needed to know that you're okay. I can distract myself while you talk to your family.

No. Wait. Stay. I need you close. She reaches out to connect with the sense of him that is with her inner being. Her hand closes on itself like she can feel him holding it.

Whatever you desire, my lady.

She can't stop herself from smiling at the title of respect that sounds more like a term of endearment when he says it.

"Fly? Are you okay?"

"Huh?" She looks up to see her brother shaking her knee, his eyes wide with worry.

"You looked like you were having a conversation in your head."

There was too much being revealed already; sharing about the mind-link with her brother could wait for another day. She steels herself and then looks at Senice.

"What's the hard question?"

Senice slowly closes his eyes, his face grimacing in pain. When he looks at her again, his eyes have a tiny hint of red that only a Kaliah would notice as he tries to keep his rage at bay. "What happened two days ago. After the gym. That wasn't the first time, was it?"

Tears overwhelm her eyes, blurring her vision, and threaten to spill. "Senice." Her voice shakes. "I didn't want to tell you. I didn't want you to confront him."

The red in his eyes blooms brighter. "Dear one." His voice is soft and strained. "It is my job to protect you. How long?"

She hesitates for a moment and sighs. "Two and a half years."

Senice's fists clench. "The ice skating accident. That was

the first time? Your twelfth birthday. Gods."

She nods her head in affirmation. The smell of anger and grief lies heavy in the enclosed space. Tears run down Fennec's face. Her heart hurts for him. She leans forward and brushes a droplet off his cheek.

"Don't cry, dear one. I'm okay." This lie is necessary for herself as much as for him. She needs to believe that she's okay, or she'll go insane.

Fennec grabs her hand and grips it tightly. She leans against him. The three of them remain quiet. Exhaustion overtakes her again, and she begins to drift off. Before she falls asleep, she feels the need to tell Lord Thyde where she'll be.

We're going to Halaa.

I know. I'll see you soon.

54

Training (Flynae)

Cellyna was over the moon excited to see Flynae. It was very overwhelming for her after everything else that had happened recently. As soon as was polite, Flynae escaped to the music room with Fennec.

The room had gradually accumulated more instruments and recording equipment over the years. The Kaliah siblings spent as many hours as they could in there playing, singing, and mixing.

After the sun went down and it was nearing time for bed, Flynae and Fennec hopped onto the roof, laid up against each other, and stared at the stars in silence. Sometime after she fell asleep, Fennec carried her to her bed.

Flynae woke up alone in the middle of the night out of breath and dripping sweat from a nightmare. She couldn't stop shivering until she toweled off and changed her clothes.

The bed looked scary and uninviting when she returned to it. Rather than get back in, she grabbed a blanket and a pillow and curled up on the floor. The rest of the night passed in short bursts of fitful sleep.

When the floor got too uncomfortable and the ability to rest seemed to be slipping further away from reach, she got up and got dressed. Her closet was full of amazing dresses. Both Senice and Cellyna like to collect them for her. Halaa was the only place she felt safe enough to voluntarily wear one so they were what she primarily wore when she was here.

The one she chose to wear was new. It was a floor-length white dress with butterfly sleeves, gold and green threading, and a matching belt at the waist to hold her lifesword. It felt amazing to finally wear her lifesword again; she kept her favorite one, which she had carved out of a cherry branch, at the ranch. After getting dressed, she brushes her hair and pulls the sides back into intricate braids.

When she hears Senice get up and go downstairs, she tiptoes down to be with him.

"You're up early, dear one," he says when she enters the room. Then he turns and sees her and stops. "You look stunning."

"Thank you." Her cheeks flush.

He pours her a mug of tea from the always-hot faucet.

"Thanks." The steamy cup is comforting in her hands. She follows him out onto the porch to watch the sunrise.

"How are you feeling? You don't look like you slept well."

"Sleep?" She laughs. "What's that?"

"I was hoping you would feel up to training today."

Her stomach clenches at the thought of the reason for the training, but she resolves that she will use that as fuel for the day. "I am. I'll do as much as I can."

He touches her arm so that she looks at him. "Don't push yourself so hard that you jeopardize your ability to recover. Your body is still healing. Be gentle with yourself."

She nods, but she knows she doesn't have the luxury of pacing herself. Neither Eksar nor Seko are going to be gentle with her. She needs to become strong enough to protect herself.

After a light breakfast, the three Kaliah head to the arena. What started as just a covered horse riding arena now doubles as a physical training facility. The column supports had been transformed from plain wood to works of art that looked like real trees straight out of a fairy tale. The underside of the roof looks like a real canopy of trees.

The morning passes with Senice coaching and instructing Fennec and Flynae through some fencing.

After several hours, Cellyna brings out a tray of fruit, nuts, and fresh lemonade for them. Flynae doesn't miss the way Cellyna glances at her before shooting Senice a glare. Senice gives a slight nod.

"All right. Take a break." He scans the area by the landing pad before turning back to the young Kaliah. "Please eat something, Flynae. There is still a lot of daylight left."

Flynae had struggled to choke down anything for breakfast. Sitting at a table to eat was difficult. Her skin crawled as she thought about how many times she had sat across from Eksar and felt his eyes on her.

She sighs and takes the dish of berries that Fennec, knowing they are her favorite, shoves into her hands. After eating a few, she sets the dish down and scrolls through her notifications on her comm.

"Oh, gods." She presses a hand over her eyes.

"What's up?" Fennec peers to see what she's looking at.

"Will's just trying some new way to communicate with me."

"You guys aren't talking? What happened?"

She closes her eyes and rubs her forehead. "He-."

"Fell in love?"

She nods. "Close enough."

Fennec puts his arm around her shoulder. "I'm sorry. We all knew it would eventually happen. No human can resist a Kaliah forever."

"I know. I just never wanted to hurt him."

Fennec bumps her arm with his. "What did he send?"

"Songs."

"Songs?"

"Yeah. We have shared playlists that we add music to that we want the other to hear. He created a new one and sent it to me. The playlist is called, 'How I'm Feeling'." She shows him the screen.

"Okay. What are the songs?"

"I Miss You. Romeo and Juliet, the one by The Killers. Just Another Girl, also by The Killers."

"Romeo and Juliet? Brutal. I don't know the last one."

"It's a good song." She starts playing it on the outdoor speakers. "Well, I liked it before. Now I'll forever think of Will when I hear it."

After they listen to the first verse and chorus and the music becomes more lively, she says, "This would be a really fun song to dance ballroom to." She stands up on her toes, increasing her height by four and a half inches as if she were wearing heels and takes Fennec's arm. He assumes a dance pose with her and follows her steps.

By the end of the song, she's belting out with the music as they dance. When it ends, she laughs and hugs his neck.

"That was great. Though we need to get you some platform shoes." When he frowns, she holds up her thumb and index finger a little bit apart. "Just like two inches. I'm almost the same height as you right now."

"Yeah, well, you like your boyfriends tall," he teases.

"Will is not my boyfriend."

"Okay, I'll give you that one. But what about him?"

She turns to follow Fennec's gaze when she feels ice-cold fingers of dread grip her torso, and her knees give out.

55

Fortitude (Flynae)

Flynae cries out as she's transported back to being four years old and watching the human who approaches her now advance towards her father with his lifesword in his hand. She sees him swing and cut into her father's body. Issiah falls to the ground in painfully slow motion. Trying to run to him is like trying to run through waist-deep water. Her chest tightens, and air comes with great difficulty.

After what feels like another lifetime trapped in the same nightmare, the present moment returns to her awareness. She's sitting on her hip on the ground, Fennec's arm around her. Senice kneels next to her, smelling of concern and confusion.

The scent that hurts the worst is the sadness and regret that flows from Lord Thyde as he stands near. She sees herself through his eyes, feels his desire to gather her into his arms, and covers her face with her hands in mortification. The weight of all three of them focusing on her is staggering.

"Gods. What just happened?" Fennec asks, maintaining his hold on her.

Lord Thyde sighs. "My footsteps take her back to when she saw me kill Issiah."

"She saw that?" Fennec's arm tightens around her.

The pain of the pressure on her bruises blends and melds with the pain of the memory of kneeling over her father's body. She doesn't care. She wants to escape from the weight of their worry and her embarrassment. At this point, she'd be happier if the earth opened up and swallowed her. That would be easier than meeting their eyes and answering their questions.

"Flynae," Lord Thyde softly says her name from close by, too close to still be standing.

She looks up gradually until she sees his hand in front of her face, palm up. There is no way she can resist taking it. His fingers encircle hers causing giddy tingles to rush up her arm and into her core. Everything else fades away as he pulls her to her feet. He's so close that his heat warms her skin.

What are you doing here? She lifts her face to look into his, everything melting away for the moment.

I told you I would see you soon.

I never thought you meant coming here. Her gaze darts towards the house and back. *Does everyone know?* Her stomach twists painfully as she imagines Cellyna's response to him being here.

Yes. Cellyna gave her approval. I'm sorry you weren't told.

Flynae laughs nervously. *I'm sure that Senice didn't think he needed to tell me if he told you.* She takes a deep breath, lets it out, and lifts her eyebrows. *So....what are you doing here?*

I'm here to assist however I can to protect you.

She looks at her uncle. "This is about exploiting the mind-link isn't it?" Out of the corner of her vision, she sees Fennec's eyes widen with the new information.

"Yes, dear one."

Her jaw tightens. She looks down at Lord Thyde's boots. How was she supposed to train next to him while being perpetually stuck in a nightmare of the past?

She addresses Senice again. "How is this going to work if I go somewhere else with every step he takes?" Her hand tightens again on Kovad's so much that her arm begins trembling. His body is like a magnet to hers; it takes all her self-control to not fall into his arms. He's her safe place, at least when he's standing or sitting still. She wants to lean into that comfort now.

Senice steps closer and caresses her cheek. "It won't be easy. You aren't the first Kaliah to be trapped by a haunting memory, but I know you have enough fortitude to overcome it. Releasing the trapped emotions of this recollection will be a powerful step towards you being completely in control of yourself."

She ponders his words and nods her head. It had never fully occurred to her that there was a way through the grip of the past. "Okay. Let's do this."

56

Control Lost (Flynae)

I don't want to let go. Flynae's aware of Senice and Fennec standing nearby waiting for her to move.

I'll still be here when you do.

He's close enough that if she were to lean forward a few inches, her head could rest on his chest. He resists the urge to wrap her in his arms; it needs to be her choice.

She spends a moment debating giving in, but she doesn't know if she can let him hold her without breaking down. Instead, she lifts her chin and releases him. "Okay. I'm ready."

She takes a step and glances down as she gets her lifesword from her belt when she sees a sprig of moss on her skirt. Her throat tightens as she brushes it off. "By the gods." When she looks up, it is obvious that all three of them have seen it.

What's wrong? Kovad asks.

We– Kaliah's clothes don't get dirty unless their energy is low.

And you are running on fumes.

"Flynae," Senice says. "Please tell us when you need a break."

She nods. "I'm good."

Fennec bumps her arm with his elbow. "I called that," he mouths with just a hint of a whisper getting through, but it's loud enough for Kaliah ears to pick up.

"Called what?" she asks just as quietly.

"Boyfriend. I saw all that hand-holding."

"Fennec Erein Let, you are ornery," she responds loudly, knowing that Senice has heard them and Lord Thyde is aware of everything she is. Her cheeks burn. She looks to her uncle to continue.

"Mind-links are rare. I know of six. The one that is the most inspiring was between Aramis and Jaizana. Their ability was like none other; they were said to wield the power of the universe together." Senice's animated face shows his excitement as he speaks.

Flynae waits for him to pause. "Those were elves, uncle."

He patiently looks at her. "That inferiority complex belongs to your father. You don't have to carry everything he gave you, dear one."

She opens her mouth to respond, but she doesn't. She ponders what he's said and finds it mostly true. "Fair point. I'll work on that."

Knowing that Lord Thyde is left-handed, she takes her place at his right hand and ignites her lifesword with her energy. They face off against Fennec and Senice.

The benefit of the mind-link alone becomes apparent to her quite quickly. They communicate intentions seamlessly. The feeling is exhilarating and fuels her, making her heart race.

She imagines how they look side-by-side, a small, slender Kaliah female in a white dress next to a tall, muscular human male in black clothing.

She takes most of her initial direction from Lord Thyde. He's a brilliant strategist even when outmatched, and she moves in response to his thoughts without question.

As it becomes clear that they might actually get the upper hand over Senice and Fennec, her enthusiasm grows. Hope blossoms within her. They could be unstoppable together.

Effort becomes easier. Her fatigue dims, and her energy renews. By knowing exactly how the other person is going to move, they're able to assail in close proximity and act like a single person wielding dual lifeswords with equal proficiency.

As adrenaline floods through her veins, every sense becomes heightened. Time slows down, and their movements become even more complimentary and orchestrated. She smells his delight at how quickly they had been able to work together.

They move even closer to the other, realizing that their closeness is an advantage. Her hip brushes his thigh, and an overhead light flickers and explodes.

Senice glances up at the sparks reigning down. The distraction is enough for the next swing from Lord Thyde to knock him off balance, and he falls to the floor.

Briefly, Flynae sees the green eyes and red hair of Issiah falling to the ground, but then her vision shifts back to recognize her uncle. Her first instinct is that he is in peril.

She screams as if witnessing another loved one dying and energetically shoves Lord Thyde. He flies backward, smashing into the sideboards of the arena.

Her heart pounds in her ears; she feels like she's underwater. Breathing is difficult.

She stares at Kovad as he slowly regains his feet, clearly winded. Someone calls her name, but the sound is muffled. Something touches her arm, and she shrieks and jerks away to see Fennec staring at her.

"Flybaby. It's okay." Fennec reaches for her, but she takes a step back.

The world spins as she looks from Senice to Fennec to Lord Thyde. Every face is filled with concern and sympathy.

Her vision blurs with threatening tears as she continues to look at Kovad and feel the dull, throbbing pain in his back. She can't cry here in front of all of them. She backs up, shaking her head, before turning and running.

Branches scratch at her face as she blindly runs through the nearby forest with no thought of what direction she's going. All she knows is that she needs some distance from what happened.

When she's out of breath, she falls to the soft dirt ground, grips her bruised sides, and sobs. Moments later her brother is leaning over her hugging her.

"What did I do, Fenn?" she manages between gasps.

"It's okay. Everyone is okay. No one is upset at you."

"I'm upset at me. I lost control." She sits up and allows him to hug her.

"You were so scared. I've never smelled that much fear before." He brushes some stray strands of her crimson hair back from her face. "And you're still scared. And ashamed. And embarrassed. You don't have to be, dear one. We're all here for you. Uncle Senice. Me. Cellyna. Lord Thyde. Though, I still don't understand that one. At all. But for some reason, he is here, too, and he really cares for you. Like pure affection without an angle."

She sniffs and wipes her eyes. "You really sounded a lot like Senice there, Fenn."

He laughs. "Is that good or bad?"

"Really good. He always knows the right things to say."

Fennec kisses her forehead. “Can I walk you back now?”

57

Humor Me (Flynae)

Flynae stands and looks down, noticing a green spot that seems out of place in her lower vision. The bodice of the white dress is smeared green with grass, and the skirt is covered in dirt.

"I ruined my dress." It was just one more thing on top of a stressful week to overwhelm her. "I really liked it."

Fennec takes her arm. "Senice will get you a new one."

The sun is setting as they get back to the ranch.

"How far did I run?" she asks.

"A few miles apparently."

They walk out of the cover of trees. Lord Thyde and Senice wait for them on the deck of the house. The Kaliah and the human stand when the siblings come into view.

Flynae's feet become heavy and she stops, jerking her brother's arm. "Fenn. I don't know that I can. What do I even say?"

He laughs. "You're Issiah's daughter. By the gods, you say whatever you want."

She rolls her eyes even as she rewards him with a smile.

"That's much better. Come on." He leads her forward.

She sees Senice notice the stains on her dress with sadness in his eyes, but most of her focus, as they approach, is on Lord Thyde. He doesn't take a step toward her, but his body is tense with restrained desire to go to her and embrace her.

She hesitates again, a few steps away from the porch steps. *Why do you smell so distraught?*

Because I don't want to ever watch you run away again. If you need to run, I want you to run to me.

Shivers rush over her skin. *Even now?*

Especially now.

She rushes up the steps, almost tripping over her skirt, and falls into him. *I'm so so–*

No, no, no. No more apologies between us. Remember? He holds her as tightly as he dares.

But this is something new.

It doesn't matter.

All too soon, she moves back from him and turns to Senice. "I think I'm ready for that break."

He smiles and places his hands on her head and kisses her forehead. "Cellyna has dinner prepared. Are you ready to go inside?"

At the thought of Cellyna, Flynae's stomach tightens and flops. How is she supposed to face Cellyna and Cellyna's ex-husband in the same room?

Senice puts his arm around Flynae's shoulders and turns to Fennec. "Would you get your sister a glass of that herbed wine we just made?"

When Fennec returns, Flynae takes the cup. The smell isn't the most pleasant, but she knows the plants used will help to calm her. "Thank you." She takes a sip. It's earthy and musty but not terrible.

The backdoor opens startling Flynae, causing her to add red wine to the stains on her dress.

Cellyna appears in a lit doorway. She gasps when she sees Flynae. "What happened to you, Fly?" She gives Senice a slight glare. "What did you guys do?"

The smell of cooking food as they enter the cool conditioned air of the kitchen assaults Flynae's nose and makes her stomach tighten more.

She looks at Senice and shakes her head. "I can't. Not tonight. I'm taking my wine and going to listen to some music"

Fennec moves to follow her, but she stops him. "I'll be okay for a few minutes. Eat, brother." *It's not your fault that tables make me ill.* She heads to the music room where she can turn it up loud without worrying since it's soundproofed. She lays down on the floor and focuses on the music in order to drown any conversation she might hear through Lord Thyde's ears. Music is her favorite way to release and recharge. She gets lost in it seeing each song as a story or dance full of emotion.

After a few minutes, she feels warm water splash her chest, except that it isn't her skin that is wet. Lord Thyde is upstairs in the shower.

She knows she won't be able to sleep until she sees what she did to his back. She retrieves the arnica and heads upstairs to lean against the wall outside his bedroom door.

You don't have to wait in the hallway. You can wait in my room.

She slips inside, shuts the door behind her, and plops down into the chair. The door to the attached bath is open, and a small puff of steam floats out. She closes her eyes in her exhaustion, but that only enhances her ability to feel him washing himself, so she keeps them open.

Moments later, the water shuts off. He towels off and comes out in just lounge pants. "My back is fine, Flynae."

"Humor me?"

"Anything you need, my lady."

He sits sideways on the edge of the bed as she stands up and walks over. Her throat is tight with anxiousness making it difficult to breathe and swallow. When she sees it, she gasps.

Over the lattice of old whip scars are two distinct wide bruises across the width of his back. Tears fill her eyes, and one escapes down her cheek.

The sight before her changes to visions of the past: the horrified look on her face hours ago before she ran away into the woods, her battered nearly naked body on the floor of her basement bedroom, her on the floor of a hallway in his ship as she recoiled from his footsteps.

"No." He pushes away his painful memories with effort as soon as he recognizes what is happening. "Come here." He turns around, takes her trembling hands, and pulls her to him.

I did that. Tears flow freely down her face. *I didn't mean to.*

I know. It's okay.

When she relaxes and leans into him, he lifts her onto his lap and holds her.

58

Respectfully. Always. (Flynae)

The first thing she notices when she wakes up is the beating of a heart in her ear. The air smells sweet and familiar. Strong arms enclose her.

Flynae opens her eyes and realizes she's in his arms, on his lap, sitting up, her head on his shoulder in his bedroom at the ranch.

His arms tighten around her as he wakes from a doze. *Good morning.*

"It is morning. I didn't mean to–." She has no words to finish her sentence as the previous evening comes to her recollection.

"I wasn't about to move you when I knew you were sleeping soundly."

Did I keep you up?

Hardly. I fell asleep shortly after you did.

She inhales deeply and presses her face into him, wanting to capture every essence of the moment. Sleep had become increasingly more difficult for her lately, and he had created a safe space for her to rest.

Her keen hearing picks up the sound of Cellyna's feet entering the kitchen on the floor beneath them. Cellyna passing by in the hallway outside the room was what had probably woken Flynae. Senice was already downstairs. Cellyna pulls out a chair and sits down across from him.

"Did you know that Flynae slept in Kovad's room?"

Flynae's body tenses, wondering how her uncle will respond.

"Yes." Senice sounds calm and unconcerned.

"That's it? You aren't worried? He's more than twice her age?"

"I know that Flynae went in there because Lord Thyde was injured during training yesterday. I know she started crying. He comforted her. She fell asleep and got the best sleep she's had in quite a while. I feel no unease about it."

"That is quite some hearing you have," Lord Thyde remarks, having heard everything Flynae just had through the mind-link.

She laughs lightly. "Yeah, well, it's not always the most fun to eavesdrop on others' conversations." As she relaxes into his warmth again, she remembers why she had come to his room last night. "Your back. You slept against it all night."

"I didn't even notice it after you fell asleep."

"Still. May I see it?"

"I wish you wouldn't torture yourself about it."

"It may be more torturous if I don't. I'll be spending all day wondering."

"In that case, then yes."

She closes her eyes and drinks in the moment one more time. *I don't want to move.*

His arms squeeze her in response. He doesn't rush her.

A few minutes later, she huffs and forces herself to stir. He watches her get up and frowns in confusion as he realizes she looks different than she had last night.

"How did your hair go perfectly back into its braids?" When she looks through his eyes, she finds not a strand out of place.

"Well, it wasn't supposed to get messed up in the first place. It only did because I was tired."

His gaze lowers from her face. "Your dress doesn't have a spot on it either."

She looks down and sees the white fabric looking brand new. "Okay. That's weird. Though I've never really gotten a dress dirty like that before."

"So it might be normal for a Kaliah?"

"I don't think so. I've never had my hair or clothing just fix itself before. Let me look at you."

He sits on the edge of the bed again. She braces herself and then moves to look at his back.

Her breath catches in her throat at the sight of his skin. There isn't a single mark on it, not even the old scars. She reaches out and runs her fingers across his shoulder blades as if she can't believe her eyes. His skin is smooth and blemish-free.

"By the gods. What?" She feels his presence in her mind, seeing what she's seeing and feeling just as baffled. Her hand and gaze move to his shoulder where she'd remembered seeing more scars last night. Next, she examines his bicep that last night had a mark like a whip had wrapped around it. His chest and cheek were missing all traces of old wounds as well.

Her hand drops from touching his face as she remembers herself and realizes how much she had just fondled him. "That wasn't solely an excuse to pet you. I wasn't trying to take liberties."

"I know. I didn't think you were. You were reacting instinctively knowing that I wasn't going to take advantage of a fourteen-year-old."

Her eyes narrow slightly as she searches his face for meaning. "Is my age the only thing stopping you?"

"Of course not. I don't ever want to hurt you, Flynae." He sighs. "Though I think there will come a time in the future when I'll need to double my daily meditation in order to continue behaving how I want to around you."

She twists her fingers together nervously in front of her torso. "How do you want to behave around me?"

The movement catches his vision; he reaches out and takes one of her hands. "Respectfully. Always."

Her heart races wildly within her as a mix of emotions overwhelms her. "We'll be expected soon. I need to go change." She knows if she doesn't leave now, it will only get harder to pull herself away from his calm, protecting presence.

He brings her hand up and kisses her fingers. "My lady." He inclines his head.

She returns the head tilt. "Lord Thyde."

Flynae hurries from the room.

59

Breathe (Flynae)

Once she's in her room, Flynae removes her dress and hangs it back up in the closet. The morning hints at the day being warmer than it was yesterday. She decides to wear a long flowy skirt and a cami. As she pulls on a clean pair of dance shorts that she always wears under dresses and skirts, she notices that her torso is without bruises.

She walks over to her floor-length mirror, holds an arm over her bare chest, and visually examines herself in the mirror. Every mark on her body is gone as well.

Look!

Lord Thyde's attention moves to seeing through her eyes. She gives him a moment to process the lack of bruises on her stomach and sides before turning around and looking over her shoulder. *What happened last night?*

I'm just as confused as you are. Would you please get dressed? I'm only human and can't keep staring at your skin.

Her cheeks flush as she realizes he's keeping thoughts of how perfect her body is at bay. *Sorry. I wasn't thinking.*

You don't need to apologize. I'm just making you aware of my limitations.

I was beginning to think you didn't have any. She slips the cami over her head and pulls on her skirt.

I have an idea. Your uncle seemed to think that you would be able to have more control over your response to my footsteps with practice. As a first step, I could let you know before I start walking.

You're going to warn me? Every time you take a step?

It's worth trying.

She shrugs. *All right.*

I'm leaving my room now.

She stands still, bracing herself for the involuntary reaction as he begins moving. Her bedroom fades to city streets. His footsteps echo as he approaches. Instead of becoming four years old again, Flynae stands upright as her current age, not allowing the memory to entirely devastate her.

Lord Thyde pauses in the hallway after shutting the door behind him. *You're doing great, Flynae. I'm proud of you.*

She grins, basking in his praise. It renews her resolve to not be overwhelmed. *Thank you.*

He takes another step.

She falls to her knees. Everything goes black.

This isn't a memory. Her head swivels back and forth but there isn't a hint of a light for her to see by. Everything is quiet, quieter than she has known in a while.

She reaches out energetically and can't feel anything. Around her feels like a void. Nothing is there.

Flynae crawls forward, reaching out in front with her arm. Within a foot or two, she reaches a wall. As she turns and quickly finds a connected wall, she begins to realize what she's missing. Everything is silent in her mind.

Kovad?

She waits.

Kovad, she thinks a bit more loudly.

No answer.

The darkness presses in. Breathing comes with difficulty. She gasps for air as the full panic of being alone engulfs her.

Kovad! she screams. The thought echoes into a void. She can't get enough air. Her chest won't expand. She wonders if this is what drowning feels like. The pain in her lungs doesn't compare to her panic that Lord Thyde isn't responding at all.

Kovad! Tears stream down her cheeks.

No one has ever broken a mind-link before. If he isn't responding, it can only mean one thing–.

Kovad. The thought is a whimper this time.

Something grabs and jerks her body. A commanding voice speaks into her ear, "Breathe."

The despair weighs heavy on her, and she feels lightheaded like she's going to fall over. With everything she has left, she yells in her head once more, *Kovad!*

Lips brush her ear as the beloved voice speaks to her again. "I'm here, Flynae. Breathe."

The darkness fades away. Traces of light appear beyond her closed eyes. Air doesn't come any easier. Her lungs are screaming.

Kovad.

"I'm with you. Breathe with me. In."

He inhales so close to her head that it cools her ear.

"Out."

Warm air caresses her cheek. When he inhales again, she tries to replicate it and catches his scent. If he's here now, then she knows she's had a vision. The hopelessness presses in again. What was going to happen that would cause silence in her mind?

No. She flails, trying to fight a complete unknown.

When he tightens his hold on her, she feels one of his arms across her upper chest, gripping her arm, and the other is over her waist, gripping her side.

"It's okay. Breathe." His head presses to hers, his lips on her ear as he speaks.

She begins to relax and breathe with the rise and fall of his chest against her back, but the silence keeps coming back to haunt her. When her body jerks with a sob, he renews his hold on her.

"I'm here now. In. Out. Breathe." His voice is calm and soothing.

As her brain begins to get the oxygen it needs to think, she asks, "What happened?"

"I can't explain what you saw in your mind. You had a panic attack."

"I was alone." Her voice is barely above a whisper.

His hold on her tightens.

"I don't want to be without you."

His arms tighten again.

The pressing loneliness pushes in. Her legs jerk as if to ward off an unseen assailant. "I can't do this–" *without you.* She can't bring herself to vocalize her worst fear.

He doesn't know what to say, not wanting to make promises he can't keep. He wants to tell her he can protect her. He wants to say it will be okay. It's all lies. This young Kaliah has a prowess that rivals his. He has little to offer her.

"Lord Thyde," she whispers.

"Yes."

She shivers in response to his breath on the side of her head.

"You're crushing me."

He releases his hands and begins to pull his arms back.

"No."

He freezes.

"Don't let me go. Not yet."

His hands return with much less force than he'd been holding her moments ago. She turns her head and sees an angry purplish mark where he'd clutched her.

"I didn't mean to bruise you."

She inhales his scent of regret. "I know. I don't care. Don't leave me." Her next breath catches in her throat. "Please."

60

Smell Different (Flynae)

Every time she thinks she has herself under control, the vision of being utterly alone in the dark returns, and her heartbeat responds by racing. Whenever she inevitably trembles in response, he renews his hold on her.

She presses her head against his. "Kovad," she says, barely loud enough for his human ears to detect.

"Yes." His breath on her cheek makes her shiver.

"I don't want to lose you."

"I will do whatever I can to remain with you, my lady."

They stay that way for several more minutes. It takes a while for her heart rate to return to normal. He doesn't rush her; he doesn't loosen his hold on her.

The loneliness of the vision returns to her recollection frequently. She finds herself bracing for something awful to happen. How many casualties will there be? Is her family in danger as well?

She's going to fight whatever is coming and threatening those she cares about, those she loves.

"I think I'm okay." Her voice shakes, betraying her. Still,

she wants to be okay. It feels like it's time to be strong.

His arms tighten around her once more for a moment as if he is loath to let her go. With a sigh, he stands and helps her to her feet.

"I think I should change again." She glances down at the dark handprint on her arm and would rather hide the mark than answer questions about it.

"I did not mean to bruise you."

She smells and feels his guilt. "I'm okay. You didn't break me." She takes a step forward, closes her eyes, and leans her forehead against his chest. "Thank you."

He gently hugs her. "Always."

She inhales his scent before pulling back. "It's getting harder to be apart. You make me feel so safe." *And I might be on my own.* The weight brought on by the potential of this presses on her again. She walks back another foot fighting the panic that has fingers around her throat.

He understands she is ready to change, inclines his head in respect, and walks from the room.

She waits until he is down the stairs before she swaps her shirt out for one that will cover her arms. While her shirt is off, she discovers a matching bruise from his other hand on her waist. Her mind's response to his footsteps was to remember being without him, and she realizes that she would prefer to be reminded of her father's death than a world without Lord Thyde in her mind.

Rather than traverse through the house and face people, she heads out onto her bedroom balcony and jumps down, landing on her hands and feet like a cat. Then she trots to the barn to visit her horse.

She sings as she enters, and her mare, Demeter, begins

whinnying at her. Flynae stands outside the stall and pets the animal.

She isn't there for long before Fennec stands beside her and shoves a bowl of homemade yogurt topped with berries into her hands. Her stomach immediately knots as she visualizes taking a bite.

"I'm not hungry."

He sighs. "You haven't been eating."

"Food doesn't sound good."

"When was the last time you had an actual meal?"

She thinks back and is surprised and horrified to realize it was the night of the banquet. She had eaten enough that no one could accuse her of not eating that night. It had been one of her victories to get through that dinner without bringing extra attention to her actions.

"Ten days ago." The words fall out of her mouth as she realizes just how long it has been since she's felt up to eating.

Fennec shakes his head. "You have to eat. Before we have to hold you down and force-feed you."

She glares at him. "Thank you for that terrifying visual."

He turns to face her, his eyes wide with worry. "What other option do we have?"

She takes a tiny taste of the yogurt. Her stomach immediately twists, and she can't hide her grimace.

"Fly?"

"Fenn?"

"Do you think you're–" His voice trails off, and he looks away.

She feels ill as she guesses the obvious end to his question. "What?"

He grimaces and shifts his weight uncomfortably.

"What?" Her voice comes out much louder than she intends.

"You smell different. Not like different emotion different, but like baseline different."

She shakes her head as she thinks back with a shudder on when it might have happened. Seko's abuse was only ten days ago. Was that enough time to change her chemistry? If not, then it would have been Eksar.

"No." She gets up and walks down the aisle closer to where the trash can stood at the end. When she is close enough, she screams, throws the bowl into the container shattering it, and brings her hands up over her face.

61

Tango (Flynae)

The irises of her eyes are bright red as she storms from the barn towards the training arena with Fennec on her heels. They climb onto the railing and sit there silently while she fumes. She can't recall ever feeling this angry in her life.

After a few moments of silence, Fennec pulls out his comm and starts a small holographic screen with it. "I've got something to make you feel better."

She huffs. "Doubtful, but go ahead and try."

"I found a human that I think you'll lust over."

Her eyes narrow, and she looks at him sideways. "Why do I need one of those?"

He laughs. "Trust me. I'm right." He starts a video playing. "He's like the top hip hop dancer on Utka."

"Never heard of it." She leans and watches, her curiosity peaked now. "Oh, gods, he's amazing," she exclaims as the performance on the screen starts.

Fennec takes a deep breath. "Yup. Called it. Lust."

"Hey, now. Is it really lust if I just want..." her voice trails off as she tries to rephrase the end of her sentence in her head.

"His body? Yes. And it's the exact same smell."

"I only want to dance with his body. Fully clothed. For artistic reasons."

"Fully clothed? You dancers are always half-naked when you perform. Case in point," he points to the video, "he's not even wearing a shirt."

She purses her lips in thought. "Fine. But it's still not lust. It's merely admiration for some sick skills."

He leans over, bumping her arm with his. "Don't worry. I won't tell your boyfriend."

She shoves him away. "First, I do not have a boyfriend. Second, I'm going to assume that you're referring to the human who is very aware of both sides of this conversation right now."

"Really?" His eyes widen in question. "Is that like an all-the-time sort of thing?"

"Every moment of every day." That empty feeling claws at her throat as the fear of losing him comes back to her.

"Isn't that weird?"

"It was."

Fennec turns back to the human on the holograph. "Okay, we've gone back around to serious. Let me show you one more thing."

She props her elbows on her knees and sets her chin in her hands. "Knock me out."

"Oh, this might." He makes a few touches and swipes. "Here we go." He makes one final touch on his comm. "The same dancer also tangos."

Her jaw falls open. "Shut up."

They watch in silence for a few moments.

She sighs. "He's good. I think the tango is my favorite. At least if we're talking off the ice."

Fennec closes his comm, slips it into his pocket, hops down, and holds his hand out for hers. "All right. Let's do it."

She puts her hand in his. "Do what?"

"Tango." Traditional tango music begins playing from the arena speakers.

She jumps down. "Do you even know how?"

"Yeah. I just watched the guy do it. You can lead when I run out of moves." He grabs her around her waist and twirls her around before taking a proper tango stance. "You said two inches right?" He lifts the balls of his feet off the ground.

She feels a twinge when he brushes the bruise. Butterflies flip in her stomach at the thought of Kovad's arms around her before the emptiness presses in with a weight on her chest. She raises onto her bare toes adding a few more inches to her height. "I did."

"I should practice alchemy more often," Fennec says with a sly grin.

"What are you talking about, brother?"

"I just turned some rubies into emeralds."

She realizes he's making a joke about her eye color returning to normal and groans. "Cheesy."

"Whatever it takes."

They dance alone for a few minutes before a small audience composed of Senice and Lord Thyde arrives. As the music ends, they finish in a low dip.

When Fennec pulls her back to her feet, he whispers in her ear. "Do I detect a hint of jealousy?"

"Your nose is off today, Fenn." She takes another inhale. "That smells possessive to me."

"Touche."

62

Possessive (Kovad)

I thought I kept myself very neutrally composed. How did you smell me from so far away?

Nose like a bloodhound. Or a shark. It's like blood in the water. What can I say? Flynae smiles at him causing him to fight his feelings and remain as uncharged emotionally as possible.

I'd never had the privilege of seeing you dance before. It was stunning.

Her cheeks turn an endearing shade of red, and she has to look away.

Do you think your brother is right? he asks.

She shivers and crosses her arms. Her mind drifts to the void, and he feels her despair. *That doesn't even matter today.*

I sense some distance. Are you pushing me away? He'd never felt resistance from her mind before.

She opens her mouth to get a full breath. *I'm not trying to. I'm just bracing. What does it mean? Do I have to continue this nightmare on my own?* She raises her feline eyes to meet his. *I'm going to fight this.*

As will I, my lady

Senice must have sensed some of her fire because he pushed them all that morning. Within an hour, Kovad was dripping sweat. The Kaliah showed no signs of tiring except for the dirt that started to creep up Flynae's skirt.

Kovad watches for Senice's eyes to register her fatigue. It was late morning when Senice called a pause. Flynae smiles and puts on a brave face before going out to the grass and lying down in the sun. Within moments, she's asleep.

The memory of Flynae nearly naked on the basement floor floods into Kovad's memory. He pushes it away thinking that she is upset and needs him only to realize that it is Senice who is struggling to keep his emotions in check. His hand is over his face, his demeanor heavy.

Kovad realizes that Senice has been hiding much of his emotions from Flynae.

"I know time is short," Senice says, "But I can't keep pushing her like this. Neither of you understand the exhaustion level required for a Kaliah's clothes to get dirty." He turns to Kovad. "Are you willing to share why she's fighting you more than yesterday?"

Kovad takes a moment to breathe and collect his thoughts. "She had a vision this morning. Either the link was broken, or I was dead."

Senice shakes his head, his emotions weighing heavy in the air. "There are no known instances of broken mind-links, not in the four millennia of Kaliah history, nor in the sixteen millennia of preserved elven history before that. "

Kovad finds himself needing to breathe through some anger. The thought of Flynae enduring her nightmare without him is maddening.

Flynae twitches and moans in her sleep.

He starts to move towards her, ready to wake her if she's having a nightmare, when Senice grabs his arm.

"She's responding to your emotions. She's okay."

Kovad looks into the eyes that carry four thousand years of wisdom and knows that Senice is right. Still, his heart rate has increased with his worry.

"What do you think it was? Was the mind link broken, or is your life in jeopardy?"

Kovad clenches a fist and presses it to his forehead. "I don't know." His voice is strained.

Senice touches his arm and pulls some of the angst from him. "What does your gut tell you?"

"I don't die any time soon. It's a ruse." As he speaks the words, he believes them more.

"Then we press forward. But how much time do we have? How long are you here for, Lord Thyde?"

Kovad looks at the Kaliah maiden lying on the ground in the sun in front of him and feels what she said earlier smelled like possessiveness. He isn't ashamed of her, her uncle, or her brother knowing how much he cares for her. "As long as I need to." He turns to Senice. "I can't let them touch her again."

63

Ruse (Kovad)

Senice takes a few deep breaths. After the third one, Kovad realizes this was partially for his benefit as he is feeling much calmer now.

"What was her response to her vision?" Senice asks.

"Fear." He doesn't know how else to explain the deep feelings they'd shared that morning. They were both afraid of losing the other.

"She's going to need your help moving forward, especially if she thinks she's putting you in danger."

He feels the ancient Kaliah's eyes studying him. "I think I'm most concerned about how hard to push the issue."

"It all depends on how resolved she is." He laughs. "She is one of the most stubborn people I know when she wants to be." Senice turns his head back to watch Flynae. "I think we should let her sleep for a bit. Is that agreeable with you?"

"Yes. I'll use the time to keep up appearances. It would be best if the Emperor didn't suspect anything."

"Speaking of the Emperor." Senice looks at him purposefully. "Are you aware of any dealings between Emperor Seko and Eksar?"

Anger swells within Lord Thyde. "I am only aware of one transaction between them so far." He clenches a fist. When Flynae whimpers in her sleep, he forces himself to push his emotions aside. He lowers his head and closes his eyes, hating to deliver this news to her family but knowing it is better if they know. At least she wouldn't have to tell them. His throat tightens as he prepares himself to speak. "Eksar hand-delivered Flynae to the Emperor for a weekend."

Fennec has been quiet and still almost like a statue watching his sister sleep for the entirety of the conversation. He turns now to look at Lord Thyde with searching eyes as if doubting his sincerity. Kovad doesn't break the young Kaliah's gaze even when the image of Flynae's beaten body in Eksar's basement blurs his vision. He forces himself to ignore it and focus.

Fennec breaks first, shaking his head, and walking away with misty eyes.

The sadness coming off Senice is almost unbearable for the human; it feels like a deep hurt to his soul. Lord Thyde channels it into an easier emotion for him: rage. His body shakes as he asks the question that's been bothering him for a while now.

"Can you explain to me why we haven't hunted down Eksar and killed him already?"

"First, it would require more than just the two of us to accomplish that. I don't possess the strength of a warrior. You wouldn't stand a chance unless we discovered how he and Xarvaxis weakened Issiah."

"Who?"

"Apologies. Seko. He publicly abandoned his old name centuries ago."

While this spurs even more questions, Kovad selects the ones relevant to the task at hand: keeping Flynae safe. "Why aren't there more Kaliah willing to help protect her as a royal?"

"Because Eksar is working for Seko. He's under the dark elf's protection."

"Then we go after him first. Cut off the head of the snake. Eliminate Eksar after."

Senice sighs. "You don't understand who Seko is. No one stands a chance, even if we gathered an army of Kaliah to face him. We're missing a Monarch."

"Fill me in then."

Senice gazes off. "What do you know about the history of the Kaliah."

Lord Thyde takes a moment to think before answering. "As far as elves are concerned, the Kaliah are a new race, only a few millennia old." He remembers what Flynae told Will that day after she'd gotten out of the hospital for the first time. "They were created by a sorcerer who somehow combined their DNA with a breed of giant cats."

Senice turns his piercing feline eyes on Kovad, making the human shiver from the intensity. "That sorcerer, was-is a dark elf who currently calls himself Emperor Seko."

The news hits Kovad hard, taking his breath away. His immediate liege is capable of much more incredulous things than he'd ever imagined. And this complicates things immensely.

Senice continues. "More than four thousand years ago, Xarvaxis captured hundreds of elves. He spent centuries experimenting with them and night stalkers. The Kaliah were the first generation that survived. Most of the rest weren't viable. Though a few violent variations escaped and were eventually hunted down and eliminated."

"What was his intended purpose?"

"To create a lethal, bloodthirsty army of beings to serve him. Seko only ever seeks to rule and destroy. That is the nature of the dark elves."

Kovad frowns. "What changed then? How was he stopped?"

"Issiah rose to the Monarchy and put a halt to Seko's darkest dealings. In the end, so many lives had been lost, that Issiah couldn't bring himself to execute the dark elf."

Lord Thyde's frown turns to a glower.

"The rejection of the elves was too much for him, for many of us, to take," Senice says. "Someone escaped Seko's captivity with three Kaliah children-myself, Issiah, and Eksar-and returned to the elven capital. No one could deny the royal blood of two of us, but the tell-tale traits had morphed. Rather than the typical raven hair and sapphire eyes, the royal Kaliah family possessed emerald eyes and scarlet hair.

"Queen Elenara, the Monarch at the time, wanted nothing to do with us. She couldn't bear to even look at us. The sight of us drove her insane. She locked herself in a tower. And one day-" Senice pauses for a collecting breath-"she jumped off. To her death.

"The galaxy passed the Monarchy to Issiah, Elenara's sister's son. It was only with his aid that we were able to travel East and stop Seko. And now that we are without a Monarch, the Kaliah are once more terrified of Seko. Xarvaxis."

Senice stops talking. The only sound is a rustling of nearby branches in a slight breeze.

"Okay." Lord Thyde's strategic brain won't cease coming up with questions and what he thinks are possible solutions. "Then how is the next Monarch decided?"

"The galaxy decides. When one Monarch passes, the gift-curse-whatever you want to call it-passes to someone of the next generation. That means it is either Siah, Fennec, or Flynae. Siah departed this corner of the universe ages ago. No one knows where he is. Fennec and Flynae are both too young to make conclusions about their potential. Though I would make an educated guess against it being Fennec. He's too much like me. Flynae however."

They both turn to look at the sleeping maiden.

"Flynae is very much her father's daughter," Senice says. "If it's her, then it may be years before anyone knows with certainty because of her age."

For once, Kovad's brain is silent, offering no potential solutions. "What are our options then?"

"We need to hide her from Seko. Keep her safe until we know who the Monarch is. Seko is their responsibility. The rest of us can do little against him."

Kovad huffs. "I despise inaction."

"I share the sentiment when my family's safety is at stake. These recent connections between you and Flynae offer some potential alternatives. I will admit that I'm intrigued but don't have any practical knowledge about it. Unless the galaxy is hinting at a certain relationship between the two of you. It's too soon for me to want to speak those words aloud. I would rather not raise hopes prematurely."

Kovad raises an eyebrow.

"Not yet. Not today." Senice shakes his head. "I want to be a little more certain first. Are you opposed to letting her rest today? She would push through if we asked her to, but I worry about the mental toll as much as the physical. We could focus on progress tomorrow. I don't think we have much time."

Lord Thyde doesn't need to consider the question. "Time is not on our side, but she needs some peaceful sleep. That has been robbed of her of late."

"Thank you. I sense you have her best interest at heart."

"Would you watch her for a moment?" He realizes that he doesn't want her lying there alone and vulnerable for even a minute. "I have a mobile computer in my shuttle. I'll sit next to her while I catch up on things."

"Yes, of course."

When he comes back and settles next to her on the blanket, Senice leaves them alone.

Kovad spends a few minutes watching her sleep before he's able to tear his eyes away and focus on something else.

Hours pass.

Movement out of the corner of his eye catches his attention. She stretches as she wakes up, arching her back, her hands above her head, toes, and fingers splayed. Then she opens her eyes, looks up, sees him, and smiles.

His heart hurts and swells with joy at the same time.

She starts glancing around, her forehead wrinkled in confusion. She sits up and turns to look at the position of the sun just above the treeline.

"What? I slept all day?"

He turns off his screen and sets his computer aside. "You were tired."

"I was still keeping up." Her voice is a mix of pout and melancholy. She absentmindedly pulls her crimson waist-length hair over one shoulder. "Oh, gods," she exclaims as if she had just discovered it was crawling with bugs and begins madly picking at it.

"It's just grass, Flynae." He reaches over and pulls off the couple of pieces he can see.

When she sighs and drops her head, he searches her mind

for the meaning and finds that this is just another form of her failing.

"Hey." He places a hand over hers. "No one thinks you're failing. We're all impressed."

She turns her head slightly and glances at him out of the corner of her eye. "You're impressed?"

"Yes." His hand grips around hers. "Very much so."

She draws up her knees and rests her head against them, resisting the desire to climb into his arms. At this point, if he would let her live there, she would. He can't help but think of how tiny she looks all huddled up.

They both look up at the sound of a door closing. Senice stands on the back patio holding a mug in his hands.

They stand up and walk over to the house together. She crosses her arms for warmth and self-soothing. Fennec comes out with a robe and puts it around her shoulders.

"Are you coming inside for dinner?" Senice asks her when they reach the porch.

"I'd rather not," she says just above a whisper.

"I didn't think so." He hands her the cups he's holding.

Flynae looks down to see it's filled with a yellow liquid. One inhale tells her it's butternut squash soup. "This isn't wine."

"Food first, dear one, and then wine."

She holds the warm container in both hands and sits down on the porch glider. "What if I promise to eat it? Can I have wine at the same time?"

Senice laughs. "Yes. I guess that is fine."

She smirks as if she has just won a little game.

Senice turns to Kovad. "Would you care for a glass of wine, Lord Thyde?"

Flynae looks up at him, her eyes wide and bright. *Will you have a glass of wine with me?*

I don't drink.

She drops her head, not willing to press further. Senice is turning away, when Kovad replies, "Yes. I will."

The small smile that graces her face solidifies to him that he has made the right choice. He sits down near her on the glider leaving a few inches between them.

You aren't going in?

I'm not leaving you.

64

Piano (Kovad)

Kovad and Flynae eat their dinner, just the two of them, out on the porch swing in silence. He senses that she's fighting a low level of panic. Her mind is elsewhere, wondering, worrying about the future. He's pleased that she finally ate something, having been unaware that she hadn't eaten in so long.

They've both been finished for a few minutes when she stands up. "I'm going to go play some piano. You are welcome to listen if you want. Or not. Completely up to you." She's used to people asking if they can watch her perform and has learned to preemptively give permission.

"I would love to." He stands and follows her.

Senice, Fennec, and Cellyna are inside around the table conversing after dinner.

"Fenn." Flynae meets her brother's eyes and tilts her head.

He hops up, understanding her meaning.

"Are you playing?" Cellyna asks, her face giving away her hope.

"Yes, ma'am." Flynae pauses for a moment to answer before

continuing to the music room. She grabs a chair on the way and sets it beside two others near the wall facing the piano.

Is this where the audience sits? he asks.

That is where the audience has chosen to sit. You may sit or stand wherever you like.

He takes a seat on one end of the row of chairs. Senice sits in the middle between Lord Thyde and Cellyna.

Flynae takes her place behind the piano while Fennec stands nearby with a guitar. As soon as she sits down, Flynae transforms. Her nervous energy is replaced with one of confidence. All emotional walls fall away. She holds herself with perfect posture and pose.

Kovad realizes that what he is seeing is similar to how he would imagine her being if she had never been abused so horribly.

She turns to Fennec. "It's your turn to choose the warm-up game."

"I've been waiting 380 days for this one," he says with a grin.

A pang of sadness forms deep in her gut at the realization that it's been so long since she's been at the ranch and able to hang out with her family. The emotion doesn't touch her face. "Which means you've had more than a year to come up with something better. This should be good."

"Cheesy rock ballads." Fennec delivers his idea and waits with an expectant look on his face for her reaction.

"Define cheesy."

His eyes dart off to the side in thought. "Um. Eighty-five percent of the songs Cellyna listens to." His grin widens.

Flynae's mouth falls open at Fennec's brazen dig at the woman. "Rude." She turns to the female human, "We love you

Cellyna," and makes a kissing motion in the air towards her.

Kovad watches Flynae take a breath and sees the corners of her lips lift. The sweet emotions were one of the reasons the Kaliah maiden enjoyed having people watch her.

Flynae turns back to Fennec. "Got it. You ready?" When her brother gives her a nod, she responds, "Faithfully."

"Bed of Roses," Fennec replies.

"Nice choice." She begins playing the song she selected. Whoever picked the first-round theme went second.

Fennec accompanies her on the guitar.

Flynae closes her eyes and her mind becomes a place for the song to play out as if she were living it. The emotions become real to her. They consume her and provide an escape. This is the only time that it is safe to feel strong emotions on a deep level.

Kovad is blown away by her singing voice. Her chest voice is warm and mature. She's never looked as adult as she does now. His desire for her swells as he listens; her voice is intoxicating; and he has to take a moment to remind himself how young she is.

Flynae watches her brother when it is his turn to sing; but when his song is over, and she begins singing again, she closes her eyes immersing herself in the emotions of the song.

She sings a love song for her second pick. Her face and body move and emote with the song as if she is living it, feeling it.

Lord Thyde finds himself struggling with jealousy as he observes her, wanting her to feel that way around him. He realizes that he will do anything for her, including giving up the position he has worked for his entire life. All of his existence means nothing if she isn't his.

The song comes to an end. Flynae smells the air. Her eyes

open and meet his. She smiles.

In that moment, he realizes that she understands the effect she has on those who hear her sing, and she thrives on it. She wants the strong emotions.

Her gaze moves from him to where Cellyna was sitting. That chair is now empty. Flynae's forehead wrinkles in disappointment as she turns to Fennec.

"Already? That was barely one song."

Fennec returns the look. "That was pretty intense, Flybaby."

Flynae looks up as she listens. Her ears detect that Cellyna is up in her room. "Sad."

"Well," Fennec says with feigned nonchalance, "one human down, one to go, right?"

"Fenn!" Flynae grimaces. "The point isn't to chase anyone off." She shakes her head and begins playing again.

Every time that Lord Thyde allows himself to relax and enjoy listening to her sing, his emotions run wild. It doesn't help that her face and body are so expressive. If she is singing about something sad, her shoulders tense and her face looks pained. When the song is about being in love, her face has a look of ecstasy, her back arches, her soft notes are even more breathy, her low notes more needy.

Every emotion that she immerses herself in floods through his body as he listens. She's completely oblivious of her effect on him except for brief moments of transition in between songs.

After a little more than an hour, she stops and closes the piano cover. As she stands up from behind the instrument, she appears to shrink back into the scared teenager who is overwhelmed by trauma. His need for her is no longer something she can grin about and causes knots to form within her instead.

Without warning, she hurries from the room and runs up the stairs to her bedroom.

65

Decisions (Flynae)

She shuts the door behind her and slides her back down it, her hands over her face. Playing the piano and singing were times when she could feel emotions that were too big for her. Today, the emotions remained after she'd stood up, something that hadn't happened before.

These blissful feelings were how she always felt that the love she wanted would feel, but they were tormenting now. The emptiness from her vision that morning took over and choked out the warmth and passion.

His focus on her captures her attention. *I just wanted to make you aware that I was going to come upstairs and need to pass your room.*

Pass my room or come inside and scoop me up and hold me again? Oh, gods! She kicks herself mentally for not being able to control her thoughts.

Whatever you want, my lady. He takes a step and then another, moving up the stairs slowly, giving her plenty of time to adjust however she needs to for his footsteps.

No. I need to think. Giving in to his constant comfort now was dangerous. The emptiness floods into her mind. Eksar's hand closes on her throat. A small cry escapes her. She rolls onto her side, curling up into a ball. How was she supposed to survive his abuse on her own?

Lord Thyde pauses outside her room knowing that she is on the floor pressed up against the door just a few feet away. He reaches out, touching the wood panel that her back is up against. *Can I do anything for you, my lady?*

I just need a couple of minutes. I was going to come and talk to you soon if that is okay.

Yes. Whatever you want.

She spends the next forty-five minutes procrastinating and trying to figure out her thoughts. She takes out her braids and brushes out her hair which doesn't hold a single kink from being twisted for the last two days. She changes from the shirt and skirt to a cami and soft flannel pants.

When she can't think of anything else to do, she goes out onto her balcony, jumps to the ground, and walks around the house. *Is now okay?*

Yes. He's sitting on his bed, looking out his patio window, wondering what her plan is. The next thing he notices is tiny white fingers holding onto one of the porch railings.

She reaches up, grabs the top board, and pulls herself over.

Did you just jump up?

Yeah. Her thoughts sound disappointed. *I kind of missed. I was going for the top rail.*

He opens the sliding glass door for her. She enters and lowers her head when she notices that he's dressed in his typical bedtime attire, a pair of lounge pants, something that hadn't bothered her last night.

What's wrong, Flynae? He finds a casual shirt in his luggage, pulls it on, and sits down on the edge of his bed.

She sits down on the floor near the closed glass door, hugging her drawn-up legs. In this position, she looks tiny and fragile.

I don't know if I can do this. She rests her head against her knees and stares at him with her large feline eyes. The empty vision replays over again in her head.

His next thought is to join her on the floor and comfort her, but she slightly recoils at just the understanding of his intention. *I'm not afraid to die. At least this way it would be in sacrifice for that which means the most to me.*

His mention of dying feels like a weight sitting on her, crushing her down. Her stomach turns. *But I need you alive.* She turns her head to press her face against her legs. *What is the point of any of this if your presence isn't my reward at the end of making it through another day alive?*

She jumps to her feet, unable to sit still with the nervous energy she's feeling, and turns to the slider, barely stopping herself from running away again. *And if you don't leave me soon, it's still going to happen in sixty, seventy years? Not even a century. And then I have to figure this out on my own.*

Her misery is thick and leaves him feeling frozen in place. She's bracing, waiting for each caress from him to be the last one.

He understands that she's struggling with his humanity. His life span is but a speck compared to how long she could live and have to remember their connection. How is he supposed to argue with that?

"I'm sorry," he whispers. "I'm going to fight to spend every moment I can making you happy and keeping you safe."

She presses her forehead against the cool glass of the door. "I was afraid of that. Exhilarated, but afraid. I'm going to go for a walk."

66

Finale (Flynae)

The moon is out and provides enough light that she can see almost as well as if it were still full daylight. The air has a slight chill, and she wraps her arms around herself for warmth.

Her hand presses against the bruise on her side. The feel of his arms around her holding her tightly and his breath on her cheek returns to the forefront of her mind. She squeezes her waist bringing back some of the pain from that morning.

Why are you hurting yourself? He'd meant to leave her alone and respect her privacy, but the throbbing ache in her side that she was perpetuating caught his attention.

Because it feels good. It reminds me of you. You should bruise me more often.

Excuse me?

She laughs aloud, breaking the quiet stillness of the trees around her. *If the reward for the pain is feeling you hold onto me that tightly, then I would accept fresh bruises daily.*

I'm not sure I could purposefully mark you like that.

What happened to the 'whatever I want'?

If you decide to quit pushing me away, then I'll reconsider your request.

Deal. She brings her mind back to the peacefulness of the woods at night, the crickets chirping nearby, the occasional hooting of an owl. All the nocturnal animals and creatures greet her with their sounds as she passes. Her presence belongs there among them, and they know it.

The cool grass and dirt refresh her bare feet. The gentle breeze plays with her hair and caresses her skin. This is what she wants. This is where she belongs. If she could only capture this space and time, she could be happy.

Her mind returns to the decision to be made. One of the factors that carries the most weight is Senice's reaction to Lord Thyde. Why does her uncle trust the human implicitly, especially given his relationship history? There must be something he knows that he's not sharing. But what could it be? How was she supposed to make a smart choice without having all the information?

What are the other options? There must be Kaliah looking for Siah during the past decade. It's a logical assumption that he's the next Monarch. If no one else has found him, how is she supposed to? Gods, even Seko must be looking for her oldest brother with the intention of finding a way to kill him next.

She audibly groans and scrubs her face with her hands. Siah doesn't know about her and doesn't know that he's needed.

Her body responds to the thought of Seko by shuddering. She's suddenly really cold. The air around her is not only chilly but also oppressive and heavy. It feels like the appropriate atmosphere to consider the third option.

If the current timing isn't right for them to stand against Seko and Eksar, then she must endure for a while. The torment she receives at their hands affects Lord Thyde as well. Is it fair for her to keep using him for relief? What if she did try to increase the mental distance between them?

No. He can't stop himself from responding now.

I thought you were letting me think.

I am. But I noticed my name. You need my cooperation if you want space. I can't do that, Flynae. I won't let you go through any of it alone.

She sighs and grips the dark purple mark on her upper arm. *All right. I won't ask that of you.*

The air becomes even denser. Her heart beats faster as breathing becomes more difficult.

Oh, gods! Eksar is here. She won't lead him back to the house. That would put them all in danger. She begins running further into the forest.

Kovad jumps from his bed, where he had been resting, unable to sleep until he knew she was back safe, and calls into the hallway for Senice.

Flynae pauses after a sprint for her struggling lungs to recover and glances around. From behind her, something glints in the moonlight. Two yellow eyes advance on her.

She freezes. Terror grips her spine and holds her feet to the ground. She fights to regain control of herself and begins running again.

A great wave of energy slams into her from behind and sends her sprawling to the ground. Eksar doesn't let her up, as he marches toward her. His eyes morph from gold to red.

"You thought you could just leave?" When he reaches her, he kicks her swiftly in her stomach knocking all air from her lungs.

She draws her legs up, trying to recover and protect herself.

He reaches down and pulls her up by her throat. His fingers squeeze the sides of her neck.

The world around her dims as blood flow to her head is cut off.

Everything goes black.

Also by Tirzah MM Hawkins

The Party is on Ream!!

If you've ever wanted to hang out and chat with an author about their stories, then you definitely need to join my Ream subscription. Why is it so great? I'm glad you asked.

Ream is where I host my private community for my fans. Feel free to follow me and just consume the free stuff which includes reviews of the books I read and certain free stories.

Or dive on in and sign up for a book box-level subscription. Every quarter, I send out a book box filled with signed books, fun items that I picked out or had made for you, and an item that I made or painted. That last thing used to be a paint pour, but I'm branching out into resin and other fun things.

You and I can dive deeper into my stories on Ream. Readers can leave comments on individual paragraphs as they read. I'll read those and respond when I have something to say back.

Want to dip your toe in? I made a custom code for you. ONEFREE

Enter that code when you sign up to get your first month as a Citizen or Courtier in my Ream realm for free. How does it get better than that?

I don't know, but it will. Especially if we keep asking.

I hope to see you on Ream. Find the link for it here: TirzahMMHawkins.com.

If you aren't interested in my subscription, then you can still find the links to everything that I've written and published at TirzahMMHawkins.com. That's the hub to find everything that I would like you to find.

9 798224 538430

Printed by Libri Plureos GmbH in Hamburg,
Germany